TIMELESS

A Short Collection
of Short Stories

SUSAN CROSS

CoffeePot
Press

TIMELESS
A Short Collection of Short Stories

Edited by Kathleen Byrne
Cover design by 100covers

Published in Canada by CoffeePot Press

ISBN Electronic   978-1-7779063-2-0
ISBN Paperback 978-1-7779063-3-7

Dedicated to Michael, my soulmate in life

BOOKS BY SUSAN CROSS

Timeless, a Short Collection of Short Stories, 2023

Double Crossed,
A Lucy Christie mystery, 2021

Canada: https://www.amazon.ca/dp/B09MM3LD6Z
U.S.A.:   https://www.amazon.com/dp/B09MM3LD6Z
U.K.:   https://www.amazon.co.uk/dp/B09MM3LD6Z

Watch for *At Cross Purposes*, the second in the Lucy Christie series, available early 2024

Contents

INTRODUCTION

TIME …. the greatest shape-shifter of all. At different stages of our lives, time either stretches or contracts, rather than passing in a linear fashion. It marches to a rhythm that matches our life experience and circumstances.

This collection of short stories divides time into the past, present, and future.

For many people, there are incidents from the past that unremittingly vie for attention. The past can grip us with its talons and force us to dwell on events, feelings, and relationships gone by. In *Stuck in the Dewdrop Stage* and *Hey Buddy*, a significant life event becomes centre stage, causing the protagonists to linger on that event, preventing them from moving forward in their lives.

In *Old Times* and *The Old Staircase*, memories of the past clearly demonstrate to the main characters that they have matured into a fully defined sense of self. The person they were in the past is no longer recognizable to them as they have changed so significantly.

The Stars Are Falling explores the life of a retired farmer as he grapples with finding meaning in his life, as his routines and responsibilities have been drastically reduced. He has so much to offer, but has difficulty seeing who might be interested in his wisdom.

The next section focuses on the present. In each of these stories, the characters are consumed with one aspect of their lives that severely limits their freedom to grow as individuals. In *Blindsided* and *Planting Beds*, the employment of the central characters curtails their ability to explore other avenues of their lives. But the money they are earning and the work they do form a major part of their character.

In *Tra La 123* and *Living at One*, life has presented the protagonists with challenges that are difficult, if not impossible, to overcome. These stories demonstrate how creative people can invent unusual strategies to confront their all-consuming life problems.

Joining the Club describes the efforts of a young woman to become popular, resulting in unexpected consequences. She is trying to force herself into a cultural mould that may not be a good fit for her.

The stories focusing on the future begin with *To Stay or to Go*, which describes the deliberations of two young people who demonstrate very different values when trying to make a decision that will drastically alter their future.

The last two stories are science fiction and portray very different worlds from the world we currently inhabit. *Limited Letters* describes the efforts of a philosophy professor to teach a seminar using materials no longer endorsed by government. She risks her entire career to rebel against the strict limitations the government has imposed to reduce the amount of print material and online communications.

Space Suit Soccer describes life on the planet after climate change has wreaked havoc on the natural world and societies have been forced to live underground. The population relies on time travel back to eras in which people could enjoy the outdoors; hiking in forests, swimming in lakes and oceans, viewing birds and wildlife. What happens when a society focuses on the past to the detriment of their current times?

I love short stories because they capture a quick snapshot of life that often spurs the reader to reflect on aspects of their own lives. They can be read for a short break, almost anywhere. I hope you enjoy these stories as much as I enjoyed writing them.

Susan Cross

THE PAST: Stuck in the Dewdrop Stage

Carrie gazes down the hill to the lake below. She isn't so much fixated on the grand view she's achieved by climbing this steep hill; rather, she is mesmerized by the minutiae of tiny dewdrops that cover every aspect of each blade of grass. She wonders if some small pocket of greenery has been overlooked, has not been completely covered in dew.

Most mornings she comes here just to see this field of dewdrops, to become transfixed by the sparkle of sunlight reflected on the morning dew. The sparkle hurts her eyes, makes her blink and causes her eyes to water. She has tried wearing sunglasses, but that just mutes the effect. She wants to experience this transitional time in full Technicolor, to endure both the joy and pain of the moment.

At this early morning sunrise, atop the hill of dewdrops, she feels vibrant and alive. For the past few months she has been able to fall asleep only around three or four a.m. But she still sets her alarm for five so that she can be part of the dewdrop time of day. It is a fairly short time. By six-thirty, the sun has greedily drunk all the life-giving dew and it will soon be too hot to enjoy this splendid view. Lately, she has shed so many tears she often becomes dehydrated. She wonders if she could lick up enough dewdrops during this short time to rehydrate herself. Maybe tomorrow she will try that.

This morning, Carrie tries to become part of this dawning of a new day. Dressed in a tank top and shorts, she takes off her shoes and socks and rolls down the hill, feeling the dew wash over her body repeatedly with each revolution, tumbling faster and faster as she moves down the hill. Suddenly, she notices the hill has taken over and she can no longer prevent herself from rolling. In reaction, she thrusts her leg out to the side to change the angle at which she is falling and stops abruptly, feeling the muscle tear in her right thigh. She turns on her back and lies still, immersed in the dewdrop tears from the hill and from her own eyes. She feels just a bit better, being totally bathed in tears.

Carrie considers herself stuck in the dewdrop stage of grief. Oh sure, she has been to … how many workshops on grief? Some perky young thing wearing bright red lipstick with a big smile on her face trying to inform her of the stages of grief she will move through. *How do you think we can listen to you prattle on about something you know nothing about? Are any of us smiling? Don't you even get that?*

Carrie finds solace in the fact that the dewdrop stage of grief ends at daybreak. When will she experience a normal day again? She imagines waking up, getting dressed, and going to work like the rest of the world. When will that happen to her? She has to keep believing she will recognize it when it does.

It is six months since Luke died. Somehow, six months is supposed to be a signal that the time of being immersed in grieving should end. Oh sure, it's okay to cry a bit and be sad at reminders of him, but it is time to move on, to get on with it, to witness the dawn of a new day. But this transition has not happened to her. She is fully immersed still.

It is her dreams that are most troubling. How can she still feel his body against hers, kissing and licking her? How can she be so aroused by a dream? She often awakens aching for him, knowing that this day is not the new dawn she is looking for. She has tried sleeping in the middle of the bed, but that makes her feel disoriented and somehow phony. The bed has two sides and one side is empty—she needs to accept that reality.

Carrie sits at the top of the hill and automatically flips her hair into a French knot. Luke sometimes walked behind her just to see her hair—long, copper-coloured, rippled with blond highlights—flow behind her in the wind. He said it was her best feature, that it looked like a waterfall flowing out of the knot and streaming down her back. Luke sometimes picked a flower and stuck the stem into the knot. He often picked a common flower, like a daisy, because he said her hair made the flower stand out and be noticed.

They were alike in so many ways. Both of them loved the wilderness. Being away from the bustle of the city and close to the natural world brought them a sense of inner peace. In fact, they had met at a wilderness survival course. On a group winter camping trip, they had been assigned to the same tent. Carrie had lain awake much of the night, shivering in her sleeping bag, unable to get warm enough to sleep. She believes that the moment she fell in love with Luke was when he laughed at her story in the morning, showing little obvious concern that she had struggled so hard to stay warm. Then he took her hand and drew her over to the fire after which he ensured she had a hot drink in her hand.

Although both avid readers, their choice of books tended to be quite different. However, a "read aloud" book was usually available on a side table in their bedroom. They took turns picking the book and the other could not dispute the choice unless the partner insisted it wasn't a book to be read aloud. That sometimes happened—some books were written to be read alone. Although they took turns reading, Luke usually read more of the book because Carrie loved listening to his deep, sonorous voice which could pick up the smallest detail and make it significant. Occasionally, he even read poetry, if she promised not to tell anyone else.

There were so many strengths in Luke's character that Carrie admired. He truly lived in the present, enjoying ordinary events that she might overlook. She remembers him following a monarch butterfly around the backyard to see what flowers it was most attracted to. He delighted in the evening fireflies and had invented a firefly dance that was hilarious. From living with him, Carrie realized she spent far too much time worrying about the future. She was learning how to appreciate the moment.

At work, they had both signed up for the four-year plan, receiving three-quarters of their salary for three years, entitling them to take the fourth year off. The destination was chosen with much negotiation and debate. They finally settled on a remote site in northern Ontario, a perfect setting to create their own little Walden, to become self-reliant and learn how to dance to the Earth's vibrations.

They had been married for five years when Luke died. It happened only a few months before departing on their year-long adventure. Carrie so regretted their decision to delay having a family until their year on the land had ended. Careers had prevailed over family.

But the affair changed everything. It filled the space between them, so there was no longer room for respect and regard. They tried to let it go, telling each other it was in the past and they were going to move on, but each felt so raw that only bitterness and pain came from their choked throats.

At marriage counselling they were told to discuss their day for ten minutes while looking directly into each other's eyes. But their days still centred on the affair and their eyes yielded no kindness or forgiveness. These trying moments were imprinted on Carrie's memory and kept resurfacing. It had been like talking to a stranger, to someone who had taken on a new and unrecognizable persona, almost like the changes that happened with dementia. They didn't have time to figure it out. When Luke died, they were strangers and no longer in love.

The contrast between the Luke she had married and the Luke of the recent past filled her with despair. This unresolved bitterness made it so much more difficult to let go, to say goodbye forever. She wonders how long she will be able to picture his features clearly in her mind. His memory is hanging on by less than a thread—it is only the chemical and electrical impulses in her brain that keep him there. One day they will degrade and photographs alone will define her memories.

The worst part of all is that she has lost the time to prove to him how deeply sorry she is and how much she loves him.

THE PAST: Old Times

Heather runs down the stairs and pulls open the front door before the echo of the doorbell fades. She wraps her arms around Jocelyn and hugs her tight. "I'm so excited you're here," she says. "It'll be just like old times."

Jocelyn pulls back in surprise. "Whoa, that's quite a welcome—kind of like our old yellow lab. Good to see you too."

There is a moment of silence as the two friends look each other over without speaking. Heather is dressed in her "best" jeans and a tee boasting Winner of the 2022 County Fair Tastiest Tart Award, with a picture of a butter tart missing a large bite. Jocelyn wears a grey linen suit with a blue silk scarf tied smartly around her neck. Both women break eye contact, looking anywhere but at each other, unsure of what the weekend will bring.

It has been two years since their friendship was put on pause as Heather moved to the country to start a family and be closer to her ageing parents. Heather remembers having laughs with her good friend and colleague; she recalls the stress of the courtroom being relieved by the bars they frequented after work. *We just need to get to know each other again*, she thinks.

As Jocelyn tries to pull her hard-sided suitcase over the doorframe of the century-old farmhouse, Heather takes her carry-on and asks her about the train trip down from Toronto.

"I love travelling first class on VIA, don't you?" Jocelyn replies. "You can actually have quite an enjoyable meal and a glass of wine, and, of course, I could get some work done at the same time. So lucky not to have someone next to me who wanted to bore me with their life story."

"Here," Heather says, reaching for Jocelyn's suitcase, "I'll help you carry your bags up to your room."

As they reach the second floor, Heather gestures to a door down the hall. "It's the second room on the left. Why don't you get changed into something more comfortable? We'll have some tea and then go out and explore the town."

Jocelyn stands at the door to her room, looking at the worn wainscoting lining the hallway. "When you told me you had bought an old farmhouse, I didn't take you quite so literally. This place really is old."

Heather smiles politely and says, "I'll leave you to get settled and go downstairs and make some tea—peppermint okay for you?"

When Jocelyn returns, the two friends sit at the old pine kitchen table, the woodstove lit and warming the expansive room. Soft cushions patterned in butterflies are tied to the seats, and the salt and pepper shakers on the table are shaped like butterflies. Jocelyn, who had changed into designer jeans and a silk shirt, looked like a misplaced fashion plate in a set of chipped, everyday dinnerware.

Heather pours their tea into two sturdy mugs and settles into a chair. "So, tell me all about yourself—you and Danny still together? Living in the same place? Who is new at Smith and Rowan? Any new lawyers?"

"Dan and I are still good, but we don't see much of each other, what with the long commutes to work," Jocelyn says. "He was a tad annoyed I was coming down here for the weekend when we rarely spend an entire weekend together. I'm up for partner next year, and I'm trying to decide if that's what I really want to get myself into—the hours will be even longer." She shifts in her chair, looking directly at her friend. "Tell me, do you miss the big city?"

Heather thinks a moment before responding. "I missed the pace and excitement at first. But after two years, I've become used to the relaxed life I lead. I sometimes miss the choices you have in the city—our stores are pretty basic here. But I'm doing a bit of consulting and the rest of the time I get to be with Stacy, who is almost two and into everything. She's napping now; we'll wait until she's up and then head out."

As they walk along the main street, pushing Stacy in her stroller, the sun lights up the panorama of newly turned red and yellow trees lining the street, and with the sweet smell of cinnamon buns emanating from the local bakery and the friendly greetings of friends and neighbours, Jocelyn feels she is in a Norman Rockwell painting. It would have been a perfect setting if not for her heels getting caught in the damned quaint wooden sidewalks, with their heel catchers set every few feet apart. Caught off guard she trips more than once, cursing each time. "Jesus Christ, why can't you have normal sidewalks here?"

Heather steers her friend into Wool Tyme, a store crowded with various colours of yarn and wool representing the seven colours of the rainbow, in shades from red to violet, with more in white on offer in the centre of the store. "Do you like to knit?" she asks. "My knitting group meets this afternoon at 3:00. Would you like to come?"

"I don't really have time to knit, but I'm happy to come and watch," Jocelyn replies.

Leaving Stacy with a neighbour, Heather links arms with Jocelyn, who reluctantly complies, and they walk together in the sunshine to the community centre, carrying Heather's knitting bag with an extra pair of needles for Jocelyn.

At the community centre, the two friends enter a room in which a dozen chairs are arranged in a circle. The windows of the sliding doors at the back look over the golf course, which stretches as far as the eye can see among rolling hills with groves of trees scattered throughout.

At three o'clock sharp an older woman dressed in a Sunday-best suit stands behind a lectern and addresses the group. "Welcome to the Knitting Sisters weekly meeting. As you know, with Peter recently joining us we are changing the name of our group. His wife, Sarah, is no longer getting credit for his lovely knitting creations. We have unanimously rejected the name Knitting Sisters and Brothers, as it sounds too much like a union. Many of you have already sent in some suggestions, so keep them coming—next week we'll vote on our new name. I have a few announcements to make before our guest speaker talks about our next fundraising project: knitting golf club covers for our Christmas sale."

It starts innocently enough, with a slight giggle escaping from Jocelyn. But then, like a geyser that suddenly erupts, the giggle turns into a loud guttural guffaw, which then flows into a high-pitched full-throttle laugh that cannot be curbed. Jocelyn's eyes begin to water, her arms flail in mirth, and her head lolls up and down as she lets herself be swallowed up by her reaction to the quaint meeting.

The only sound breaking the startled silence of the room is Jocelyn's laughter. All eyes are glaring at her, with various expressions of disgust, embarrassment, horror, and surprise playing over the members' faces. The chairwoman is clearly embarrassed and unable to respond, holding her hands to her mouth, the first to look away.

Initially, Heather joins in with the slight giggling of her friend, but when Jocelyn continues in uncontrolled merriment, mixed emotions of pain and shame envelop her and she freezes in her seat. She thinks about the community she has joined and now loves, and believes she has betrayed them in some way. Grabbing Jocelyn's hand, Heather drags her across the room and out the door. Once outside she realizes her knitting bag is still inside, but she can't go back for it.

Out on the sidewalk, Heather's body seems to split into two distinct halves. Her old self can see how funny the announcement and meeting might appear to a big city gal; you wouldn't encounter this kind of thing in the city, she knew. But her new self is mortified, and she wonders how she will mend her relationship with her knitting group.

Although the entire event likely took less than five minutes, to Heather it resembled slow motion, with time, feelings, and reactions being magnified and memorable.

Jocelyn stammers a tongue-in-cheek apology as she continues to laugh. "I'm sorry I lost control (ha, ha) and that I disturbed the meeting (hee, hee). I couldn't help myself—it was too funny. Wait till I tell everyone at work about this (ha, ha, ha)."

"Why would you do that?" Heather asks. "Do you think my life is that laughable?"

"Well, you've got to admit that announcement was pretty hilarious. It's just a comic moment, not such a big deal—don't take this so personally."

They walk along in silence for a few minutes. "Why don't you get that work done that you said you had to do this weekend?" Heather says finally. "I'll fetch Stacy."

At dinner there is no further commentary on Heather's lifestyle, so starkly different from Joycelyn's. They talk about their gardens, movies they have seen, small-town and big-city politics; safe topics that reinforce the protective masks they both now wear.

In the morning, Jocelyn sleeps in late and joins Heather for brunch. "The air is so fresh out here; I slept so much better than at home. Everything smells so outdoorsy and clean. Food even tastes better."

Heather knows that this is Jocelyn's shot at an apology, but she doesn't believe it is a sincere attempt. She mentally pulls her plastic smile out of the dresser drawer in the basement where she had packed it away upon moving here and pastes it on for the rest of the stay. Yes, she realizes, this is just like old times.

THE PAST: The Stars Are Falling

Joseph lifts one foot and places it in front of the other. He repeats this motion over and over despite the arthritis acting up in his knee. "If you ignore the pain, it won't have anywhere to live," his mum used to tell him when he had injured himself on the farm. Joseph fondly remembers those days of hard labour when, at the end of the day, you could see the results of your work—the miles of fences built, the number of sheep sheared, the bales of hay taken off the field. The never-ending work that gradually wore a body out, like the drive belt on a tractor.

Joseph's body began to wear out two years ago, at the age of seventy-four. He finally gave up working on the farm and retired to a cottage up the road from his acreage. His farm is ten miles from the sea, a couple of hours' drive from Norwich in East Anglia. Most days he walks the three miles to the village pub to chat with a group of men he has known since childhood.

The group is smaller now, reduced to Eddie, Peter, and Rob. Stewie died two months ago—he had been the joker of the group.

Joseph looks over the flat farmland as he walks along under the blistering sun. He knows every mile of this countryside, all the subtle changes in a prairie vista: where the canola changes to wheat, where the water gathers after a heavy thunderstorm, where the blackberries can be found in the thicket. He sometimes believes he is closer to the land than to most people in his life.

A red lorry speeds past him, the man on the passenger side waving out the window and calling out, "Hey Joe, how's it going?"

"Don't call me Joe!" Joseph yells back as the lorry roars past. "My name is Joseph. Why don't people in this village know that? There doesn't need to be a short form for everything," he mutters under his breath, trying not to breathe in the dust cloud raised by the speeding lorry.

Joseph increases his pace, feeling his heartbeat pulse in his neck. He purposefully tries to get his exercise for the day before his noon hour dinner at the pub. He likes to think they cancel each other out. For two years now, the main event in his day has been walking to the pub to see his friends and sometimes walking back, at other times getting a ride with a friend. Today he wonders about the point of it all. Back and forth, back and forth along the same route, like the path the ants take across his storage shed.

When he first retired he had the cottage to fix up, but that was now complete. Then he started shadowing his wife, Ethel, trying to help out around the house. Finally, one day, she put down her broom and softly, but firmly, told him it was time for him to get out of her kitchen and find something to do. She had her daily routine and most of it did not include him.

Joseph reaches The Prancing Pony, wipes his brow with his red handkerchief and walks into the bustling room. After waving his arrival to his friends, he heads to their usual spot, a table close to the fireplace for cold, rainy days. Joseph stands out at six foot six. His big head atop his lean body has several small scars from bumping his head on structures too low for his height. He still wears the same coveralls he wore when he actively farmed. He doesn't feel comfortable in anything else.

Joseph sits in his chair; they all sit in their set places as if this is a kitchen table at home. He joins in the conversation concerning the plans for the fishing trip next month. It's a positive step to plan a trip and think of doing something different. Peter asks if he can bring his son along. "What would he do with a bunch of old men like us?" Joseph asks.

Joseph half listens to the same topics he has heard day in and day out for the past two years: the weather, which crops are doing well, how their kids are now running the farm with new, modern ideas. More and more, Joseph feels like an observer on the sidelines of his own farm, much like the barn owl perched on the fence—watching and commenting, with no one really listening. His son, Joseph Jr., is doing a fine job and doesn't need him anymore.

"You seem a touch off today, Joseph," Rob says as the conversation dwindles to a halt. "You're not quite yourself."

"There's got to be more to life than the daily draught, Rob. I need to be useful. Not sure what to do with myself since I turned the farm over to the boy."

Rob nods. "I know what you mean, Joseph. I sometimes sense the clock is ticking with not much happening. If it weren't for the grandkids, I'm not sure what I'd do. We've got our hands full looking after those three ragamuffins." Rob's eyes sparkle with delight when he shares the antics of his grandkids. He smells slightly of sour milk.

Joseph is proud of his two grandchildren, but they are teenagers now and not so interested in spending time with him. They don't really need him either.

Peter overhears the conversation and invites Joseph to help him work on his Massey Ferguson tractor. "I'm getting her ready for the antique fair next month—she's a beaut," Peter says with pride.

"Aye, yeah, let me know when I can help," Joseph says with little enthusiasm, but feigning a smile.

"I was the same when I first retired, Joseph, but you eventually find your own routine and putter through your day," Eddie, who is 82, joins in. "Now I spend a lot of time constructing model airplanes. I'm working my way up to the one in which my grandfather died flying during the war—that will be my final one."

As Eddie is talking, Joseph notices the pub is filling up and people are moving their chairs and pints of beer closer to their table. Feeling so lost and aimless, Joseph has not given thought to the story he will tell today. Eddie's grandfather dying in an airplane during the war triggers the memory of a story he hasn't told in a long while.

Joseph looks up and clears his throat—this is always the signal to start and the chatter dies down. "I'm going to tell you a story from when I was a boy during the war—those were hard, but memorable days." Joseph's low, warm, sonorous voice quells even the gabbiest members of his audience.

"One evening, I snuck out to the tree house just to be outside and watch the stars. Of course, you weren't supposed to be out in the night, especially under an almost full moon, but I made sure I didn't even have a torch with me. I knew the ladder up to the tree house and the wooden platform high in the oak tree like the back of my hand. The Milky Way was dancing with light and mystery and millions of stars coated the dark sky."

Joseph's eyes sparkle like the stars he is describing and his voice transports his listeners back in time to that dark night.

"Suddenly, it looked as if some of the stars were falling. And it wasn't only one star; there were several stars collapsing to the earth. I stood up, too terrified to keep watching, yet too frightened to draw my eyes away. My mum and big brother needed to see this. I jumped down the ladder and ran into the house, imploring them to come outside and see the falling stars. They turned out the lights in the house and came outside with me and gasped in dismay, trying not to call out loud even though there was no one near to hear them.

"'We've got to let the troops know what we've seen,' Kevin, my eldest brother, said. 'I'll take the back route through the fields.' The farmers had cut a narrow road through the corn and wheat for soldiers to travel safely off the main roads. Kevin ran into the darkness and my mother rushed me into the house. That night, we slept in the bomb shelter dug into a hill away from the house. We didn't see Kevin until morning. He was smiling and laughing with my mother, so I knew everything was okay.

"No one thought to tell me until I was a few years older that I hadn't seen the stars fall that night. I had watched carefully for weeks afterward for a second sighting, but I never saw the stars fall to the earth again."

Joseph has been telling stories of the county in the pub three days a week since his retirement. He no longer remembers whether some of the stories he has told are true or whether he invented them. But does it really matter? He now has an established reputation as the county raconteur and regularly shares the area's history in story format at county fairs, the library and at local schools.

"So, what's Friday's story?" Angie asks as she finishes her pint and prepares to head back to work. "I don't want to miss it. This is the best part of my day."

"Even I won't know until then," Joseph chuckles.

The crowd disperses, bidding fond farewells after having their fix of fantasy, the kind only a true storyteller can provide. The numbers have been escalating to the extent that the pub is at capacity over the dinner hour. Stuart, the pub owner, had offered to pay Joseph for his performances, but Joseph just laughed and said he wasn't doing anything worthy of payment.

Joseph leaves the pub still feeling an emptiness in the middle of his chest, like a black hole in the galaxies above; a void he can't seem to fill. On impulse, he heads home in a different direction, looping by the lake and the cluster of birch trees. He wants to try something different.

Lost in thought, he struggles to find a meaning for his life, a reason to get up in the morning. A lorry with a wide load races by him, blasting its air horn, startling Joseph out of his reverie.

The first thing that seeps into Joseph's consciousness when he wakes up at the bottom of the ditch is a dull throbbing in his right leg and head. He tries to sit up, but dizziness overtakes him and he falls back down onto the hard rocks. He turns his head and expels the remains of his dinner. He can't move his leg.

Tendrils of fear and dread creep over him until it feels as if a thick mat is suffocating him. Joseph wonders if they will find him. He has never veered off the most direct route home. He passes the time and keeps his fear at bay by recounting one story after another to himself, fine-tuning the details of his stories for his loyal followers.

Susan Cross/36

THE PAST: Hey Buddy

Ruth glanced down at her cell and groaned. *Not another text from Mom—why did I ever teach her how to text?*

Text: "Come over now."

Text: "What's Dad up to?"

Text: "Napping."

Text: "Passed out? Good. See you soon."

Text to Gerry: "Dinner late. At Moms."

Text from Gerry: "Are you nuts? Don't go!"

Ruth walked over to her parents' house despite the minus-fifteen-degree weather. It gave her time to cool off and steel herself against the unsettling and likely demeaning experience ahead of her. Pulling out her cell, she reviewed the affirmation of the day: *I appreciate the little things.* She chuckled to herself, muttering, "Yeah, the big things are pretty fucked up." She wondered why there was never an affirmation stating, *I appreciate the big things*. Maybe that was too much to hope for.

Walking in the front door, Ruth squeezed between the piles of boxes and newspapers lining the hall. As she could hear her dad snoring on the couch, she glanced into the living room. His left eye was yellowish from bruising and his hand was purple with a visible cut on the thumb. *That's what you get for drinking too much.*

Her mom was making soup in the kitchen. "Want some help with the veggies?" Ruth asked. "How do you want the carrots cut up?"

"Oh, anyway you like. Just don't make them too big, like you usually do."

Ruth took out a cutting board and gathered up the carrots. "So, what did you want me for? Computer problems again?"

"Our Wi-Fi isn't working and I want to read the newspapers on the library site. I don't know why you can't fix it so that we're always connected."

Taking a deep breath, Ruth asked if she had turned off the router. "You know I get those things mixed up—just fix the damn thing."

Ruth went into the spare room and 'fixed the damn thing.'

"Is that all?" she said when she returned. "I'll finish the carrots and then go back home and make our dinner. This soup smells wonderful."

"You might as well cut up the potatoes and celery while you're at it," her mother said, wiping her hands on her apron. "I'm going upstairs to use the computer."

Ruth left her parents' house, having worked alone in the kitchen finishing the soup. No one said goodbye or offered up a thank-you. Why expect something different?

Ruth took the long way home, walking by the lake. The full moon sparkled on the frozen expanse of water. It looked like a beautiful white wasteland. She sat on the edge of a frozen slab of ice that had broken apart at the shore and let out a long, sad sigh. The tears flowing down her face pinged on the ice below and she watched as her tears turned to ice. *Be careful of your heart*, she told herself, and continued her journey home.

Once home, she went right to her top dresser drawer. Pushing through the pile of scarves, she found the royal blue box. She opened it to see the small stiletto knife gleaming up at her. "Hey Buddy, you're still here. Good."

Hearing Gerry's voice at the doorway, she tucked the knife away and went to greet him.

"So, you survived the ordeal?" Gerry still had his parka on with his fur-trimmed hood up. At six foot five, he looked like Hagrid from Harry Potter, with his beard frozen and matted from the frigid weather.

"Yeah, not so bad. The usual," replied Ruth as she reached up and pulled on the edges of his hood down to her level, and kissed him firmly on the lips. "Now my face is dripping wet," she laughed as she turned to leave and start dinner.

Gerry pulled her close and suggested a detour to the bedroom, unbuttoning her blouse while nibbling on her ear and massaging what he called her pert little butt. "Hmm, a little appetizer, just what I need," she murmured as his hands explored her taut nipples, waiting to be admired and caressed.

As they lay on the bed, tingling from the aftershock of sex, Ruth stroked Gerry's chest and followed the outline of an anchor tattooed on his arm. "Even the bloody carrots—I can't even cut up the bloody carrots right."

"I don't know why you go over there. It never ends well, Ruthie."

Working as a team, they quickly assembled a healthy dinner. "So how was your day, apart from the parents?" Gerry asked as he ladled a big spoon of spicy Thai chicken soup into his mouth.

"I don't understand why I put up with it. It's like repeatedly going into a cave with snakes living there. You know they are likely to bite."

"You are well aware of my solution to the problem. Please come with me. I love you and need you with me, you know that."

Ruth's eyes teared up as she put her soup spoon down and stared at the table. She looked up into his eyes, hoping to relay her message clearly. "You know how important you are to me. Of course, I want to come with you. But what about Mom? What might happen if there's no one here to protect her? Australia is so far away."

"She doesn't deserve your loyalty—she treats you like a servant, not a daughter." Gerry got up, leaving his half-finished soup on the table. "Are you always going to put her needs first?" He grabbed his coat and left the apartment, clenching his fist and trying not to slam the door.

As he walked along the icy street, his breathing slowed. He regretted running out like that. Lately he had noticed dark shadows under Ruth's eyes, resembling worry clouds that forecast a storm ahead. She desperately needed to get away from her parents' toxic presence. The Ruth he once knew was slowly being gouged away. Her ability to turn her face to the light was noticeably diminishing. It had been three months since the "accident." It was then the Ruth he loved and cared for began to morph into this person fraught with worry and anxiety. Would he leave without her? He so hoped it wouldn't come to that.

Ruth dragged herself out of bed the next morning when the alarm announced six o'clock. She grabbed her gym bag and, eating a banana on the way, drove to the spinning class that most mornings woke her up and made her feel alive for an hour. As they were warming up, her friend Jody, on the bike next to her, asked, "How's it going with the folks?"

"As discouraging as ever," she replied. "Not sure there is a solution at all. Gerry and I had a spat over my relationship with them last night."

"Wanna go for a drink after work? Meet you at Buster's at six."

Ruth had opened her own flower shop, Floral Expressions, three years ago. She was finally operating in the black and had two weddings and a funeral to prepare for today. Her favourite part of the day was opening the door when she arrived in the morning and smelling the heady aroma of freesia, lavender, herbs, and the cinnamon sticks she kept at the till. It was the smell of growth, of promise, of spring. On freezing days like today Ruth kept a slow cooker of apple cider brewing for her customers to drink to warm up.

Ruth started on the bridal bouquets. Fortunately, she had talked both brides into the same flower theme, with minor variations. To form the base structure of the bouquets, she pulled out white calla lilies, stephanotis, and red roses. She began the circular motion of wrapping the floral tape around the flower stems so that it was taut and smooth. Her muscle memory took over and her fingers moved to an inner creative rhythm. Time collapsed as she immersed herself in her work, providing a legitimate excuse to avoid the difficult decision she had to make. Surprisingly, she never thought of her mother for even a second.

The entrance bell rung as Rupert came rushing in, always five to ten minutes late. "Hey Doll, I'm here, don't worry," he said as he came up to her and kissed her on both cheeks. Rupert always dressed up on Mondays, with a sharp cravat and striped vest snugly fitting over his blinding white shirt, as he knew the regulars would be dropping in to buy their weekly fresh flowers. He ostentatiously flirted with them all despite being recently married to his partner, David.

Ruth watched as Rupert moved efficiently through the store, gathering the flowers to form the individual bouquets for each customer. How could she manage without him?

She remembered the first day he had dropped in over his lunch hour. "Can I help you with anything?" she had asked.

"Picking out the right flowers is such an important decision," he had replied. "I need to think it over." Three lunch hours later, he was still thinking it over.

One day, she overheard him talking to another customer. "I'd recommend the white lisianthus with the red roses. They really complement each other." "Thanks so much, I'd never thought of that."

After the woman thanked him, Ruth went over to Rupert. "So, you know a thing or two about flowers. Have you always been interested in plants?"

"Oh yes, but I'm truly stymied right now. I'm saddled with the selection of flowers for our wedding. David doesn't really care. I keep changing my mind."

Ruth spent several lunch hours helping Rupert mull over his floral expression of love for his partner. Two weeks after the big day, Rupert quit his job and began his new career as her associate. Rupert was now both an employee and a dear friend.

"I'll bet you've been stewing over your pathetic parents. I've worked here long enough to read the signs that you've recently had contact with them. Wanna go for a drink after work?"

"Christ, is it that obvious? How can you tell? Jody knew right away at our spinning class this morning as well."

"It's your eyes—they have this sad and lonely look. You do a good job trying to hide it, but to those who love you, it's obvious."

Ruth's eyes teared up. "I guess I am a little fragile at the moment. Why don't you join us at Buster's? As long as you don't mind a pathetic parent rant."

The grandfather clock that kept meticulous time rang nine bells and Ruth unlocked the door for the customers waiting outside. The busy day would help keep her mind off her dilemma.

"Rupert, what special posy are you going to surprise me with today?" Ella Smithers asked, with a twinkle in her eye.

"I've added in blue delphinium to match the colour of your eyes," Rupert replied, pulling out her flower arrangement. "Close your eyes and smell the magnificent scent before you gaze at the most glorious bouquet you have ever seen. Remember, you have five minutes from when Granddaddy clock chimes the quarter hour to name the eight different flowers in your posy."

Rupert had significantly increased the number of regulars by challenging customers to name the flowers in their bouquets to get a 10% discount.

Ruth went into the back room and brought out a good supply of her recent invention, The Flower Sack. It was an ultra light-weight down bag shaped like a quiver for arrows. She was in the midst of patenting her invention and planned to market it to florists across North America. Realizing that using paper to wrap flowers for transport in a Canadian winter was a foolish custom, Ruth had worked with a company that produces down vests to develop her product. It could also be used in the hot summer to keep flowers cool and fresh. All of her regulars had purchased them and now their friends were coming in to buy them for Christmas presents. She could barely keep up with the demand.

At the end of a very satisfying day, she locked up the store and strolled down the street to Buster's with Rupert. She threaded her arm through his and absorbed the warmth and care he emanated on a cold winter's evening. "Thank you for taking the risk of coming to work with me. If I decide to move to Australia for a year, would you really look after the store?"

"As long as you give me some leeway for creativity, Ruth. Maybe adding a Rainbow Corner at the east end of the shop. You know I'll do my best."

Inside the bar, they joined Jody at a tiny, cramped table. "Hey, Jody. Look who I dragged along with me," Ruth said.

"Oh good. More ammunition to get this girl away from here," Jody replied, as she took Rupert's icy hand and warmed it with her own.

Ruth loved the intimate interior of Buster's. It was a comfortable, low-end bar, crowded with small tables surrounded by mismatched chairs. Strings of golden lights lined the mirrors and outlined the archways separating the three rooms that made up the bar. The walls were painted with intense, dark colours that contributed to the warm, cozy feel of the space. The smell of draught beer, peanuts, and pretzels was a favourite of hers. She ordered her pint of Beau's and a warm, freshly baked pretzel and dived right into the subject that ruled her life of late.

"So, do you both honestly think I should just up and leave for a year? I need you to be really honest with me."

They both looked at her as if she were daft. "If you have to ask us that question, you're nowhere near the answer for yourself," Jody replied, looking sad, and a tad annoyed. "To us, the answer is obvious. You deserve a life of your own."

"But if she gets hurt again and I'm not here, how would I live with myself?"

"You can't live your life enveloped in hers, Ruth," Rupert replied. "She needs to make her own decisions. You're not her bodyguard."

"Last night I had the most vivid dream. I was about eight and she was trying to teach me how to knit. She kept repeating over and over again, 'Why do you even try? You'll never succeed.' The mantra of my childhood came back to haunt me. She always finds fault in what I do."

"I can see you wanting to protect her," Rupert replied, "but remember that it is her choice to stay with him—she has the freedom to leave."

As Ruth started on her second pint, the knot of tension and anxiety that lived most days in her bowels loosened up; the relief was astonishing. Is that what had happened to her father? She had never thought of the origin of his alcoholism; it just seemed to be a part of him, like a finger or a toe. Could it capture you by adopting such an innocent gesture?

The day of "the accident," Ruth had received a text from her father.

Text: "Mom hurt. Come soon."

Phone call to Dad: "How badly hurt is she? What happened?"

"She tripped and broke her arm. It looks bad."

Ruth arrived to find her mother lying on the floor staring at the bone that jutted from her arm as if it were an art form. Her pallor was grey and her words were confused. She looked so small and helpless, lying so still and quiet. Her face appeared stunned, empty of emotion or the ability to react.

Once her mother was settled in the hospital with a cast on her arm and an IV bringing her nourishment, Ruth asked how she had broken her arm.

"It was just a foolish accident. It was my own fault."

"Was he involved? Did he do this to you?" Ruth tried to ask this in a civil voice, keeping the tone of her voice even and low in volume.

"He didn't mean to. It's not his fault; you know he'll never stop drinking now."

Ruth left the hospital and went home to get Buddy, tucking him into her front pocket. She stormed through the front door of her parents' house and confronted her father, who was sitting in his usual armchair, cradling his head in his hands.

Holding Buddy for safety in her pocket, she looked him right in the eye and said, slowly and loudly, "Don't you dare ever hurt her again. I am so ashamed of you." She turned to leave, but stepped back into the living room and said, "And don't ever speak to me again."

His eyes opened wide in surprise. He tried to speak, but the words would not come out. "Ruthie, Ruthie," was all she heard before she left the house, slamming the door.

Buddy had been her constant companion since grade nine, when she and her two best friends had convinced an older brother to go into a pawnshop and buy the three stiletto knives. "BFFs," they said as they made a tiny cut with the knife and rubbed their bloodied fingers together. Afterwards, they collapsed in a pile of giggles and friendship. They made up stories of how they would defend themselves and always feel safe. Ruth hung out with these close friends for several years, but left shortly after they started a cutting club. After a few cuts, Ruth decided she just wasn't into that. Buddy hadn't made another cut since. Hopefully, that was all the blood Buddy would draw.

"Did you know my dad was my best bud when I was younger? He was the one who teased me, who gave me giant bear hugs and took me out for ice cream." Ruth smiled and looked happier than she had in at least a month. "Hugs from my mom were rare, and she was stiff as a board when I hugged her, as if I were tormenting her. I eventually stopped trying to get a hug from her. I don't think she ever told me she loved me.

"Did you love one parent more than the other?" she asked Rupert and Jody.

"Not really," Jody said. Rupert just shook his head.

"I remember in grade six asking my father why my mother didn't love me," Ruth told her friends. "He said she loved me in her own way. By the time I started high school, I spent almost all my free time with my friends in their homes, as I no longer wanted to bring them home to meet my mother. She was so cruel, even to my friends. One weekend, she called my best friend, Betsy, a bitch for running through the living room and breaking a vase on a side table. I recall my father's drinking gradually increased, eventually reaching the point of his being drunk most nights. Unlike my mother, he was never mean, but I was so embarrassed and ashamed of him. I realize now I may have judged him too harshly. It was the accident that changed it all for me. How could he do that to her?"

"How do you know for sure your dad was responsible for her accident? Did you ask him?" Jody looked directly at Ruth, waiting for an answer.

At first, Ruth couldn't decipher what Jody was asking. "What do you mean? Of course, it was his fault."

"But how do you know that?" repeated Jody.

"Well, my mom said he didn't mean to do it, it wasn't his fault, but that still means he did it."

"But what exactly happened? If he didn't intend to do it, possibly it was an accident."

Ruth's mind whirled. Conflicting thoughts collided in her brain, making her breathless and light-headed. *Have I needlessly blamed my dad? I accused him without asking his side of the story. He tried to talk to me, but I wouldn't listen.*

"You're right, Jody. I never talked to my father about it. He wanted to talk, and I stormed out of the house. Most nights he's too drunk to talk. I'm going to head over there right now and see if he is sober enough to straighten this out. It's important. Thanks for the insight."

She gave Rupert and Jody a lingering hug. "I love you guys so much. Thanks for your support."

As she drove to her parents' house, she planned her approach. "I need to breathe deeply; I need to listen; I need to prevent myself from jumping to conclusions; I need to stay calm."

Opening the front door with her key, she tiptoed down the hall. If he had passed out, she didn't want to alert her mother of her presence; she wanted to slip back out unseen. She heard a loud moan coming from the living room. Peering around the doorway leading into the living room, she witnessed a sight she would spend years trying to erase from her mind. Her tiny, frail Mom was wielding a baseball bat in the air, directing it to land on her father's torso. He was lying on the ground, covering his head with his arms, moaning in pain. The stark realization of what likely had been happening for years shook Ruth to the bone. She had attributed her father's bruising from stumbling and falling in a stupor when drinking. With her phone in her hand, she instinctively took a video of the unspeakable act.

Ruth ran into the living room and grabbed the bat out of her mother's hands. "How can you be so cruel? How can you live such a lie, allowing me to believe that he was the abuser? I'm calling the police."

Ruth managed to stay focused and calm throughout the entire process of getting her dad to the hospital, answering endless questions from the police, and watching her mom shrivel into her act of being a helpless old woman, with no choice but to defend herself with a baseball bat. Fortunately, Ruth had the video to turn over to the police.

Finally arriving at her apartment after midnight, Ruth crept in, not wanting to wake Gerry. But the apartment was so still, so empty. A note addressed to her was lying on the kitchen table. "I now realize that you need to focus on your parents and, therefore, cannot have a future with me. Although I love you dearly, I can't live like this anymore. I've moved to Barry's until I leave for Australia. Goodbye, my love."

With tears streaming down her face, Ruth went to her dresser drawer. "Hey Buddy," she said, "I really need you now." Curling up in fetal position on the rug, she hugged Buddy against her chest. "Maybe it's time to start cutting again."

THE PAST: The Old Staircase

As Amanda raced up the stairs, her long auburn hair flew back like the steam escaping from a fast-moving locomotive. She paused, breathless, at the top, galloped into her bedroom, grabbed Bunnywinkles by the ear, and tore back down the stairs, barely aware how fast she was manoeuvring the path down to the front door. So familiar was this descent that she arrived in the small foyer sooner than she realized and almost slammed into the frosted window imbedded in the top two-thirds of the burnished mahogany door. Amanda grabbed the doorknob, fully intending to turn it and leave forever the house which had been her home for the last 14 years.

However, the view of the staircase displayed behind her in the mirror beside the door curtailed her abrupt departure. She took a deep breath and slowly turned to face the stairs, all 14 of them. The stairs were solid oak, seven steps up, a roomy landing halfway up, and then seven more steps to climb to the second story of the old house. Each step had a slight depression in it where Amanda, her four siblings and parents trod up and down, up and down, connecting the quieter area of the house to the noisy, busy living area on the ground floor. The stairs beckoned her to climb to the top one more time and slowly descend, reliving her childhood memories.

Amanda had moved to this house on Oakland Avenue when she was three. She recalled her first look up this long, now familiar staircase. She had gingerly climbed it the first time, pausing on the halfway landing, wondering if she could convince her short, stubby legs to finish the climb. As the youngest child of the household, she needed to climb the stairs quickly to claim her bedroom before the older sibs took the best rooms. But they had all crowded past her at the landing and she sat down on the tenth step, clutching Bunnywinkles, resting her tired legs.

As if in a time capsule, she now sat down on the tenth step and considered how much both she and Bunnywinkles had changed over the past fourteen years. Bunnywinkles had been loved to death. The fur had been rubbed off his right ear until his ear looked translucent, like frosted glass that revealed too much. His lucky rabbit-fur tail had long since disappeared and the carrot in his right hand was a sickly brownish-green.

Amanda reflected she was glad she had not been loved to death in the same way as her faithful companion. However, she concluded that the unconditional love that had surrounded her throughout her childhood was largely responsible for the healthy, confident, happy young adult she had become. Amanda's fingers automatically started rubbing Bunnywinkles' right ear as she whispered, "I can't believe I almost forgot you."

As she continued down the stairs, Amanda's eyes were drawn to the missing spindle on the fourth step. Over the past twelve years she had grown so used to its absence that it seemed odd to notice it now. Her foot had broken the spindle in two one day when her twin brothers, Chad and Curtis, had accidentally knocked her off the landing while chasing her in a wild game of hide-and-seek as both she and Curtis frantically tried to touch the landing, which was always base camp. Her broken toe had mended quickly.

Being the youngest of five children had its pros and cons. Physically, she was always trying to keep up with her brothers, who were three years older. She was closer to Chad and Curtis than to her two much older sisters, Sarah and Samantha, who generally tried to ignore their younger siblings and had left the family home at least six years ago. Chad and Curtis had contributed to creating her fighting spirit and her fearlessness in trying anything physical. But the sense of always trying to catch up, but somehow not quite making the mark, was indelibly woven into Amanda's sense of self.

"Amanda, what are you doing in there? Get out here or you're going to miss your train."

Amanda ignored the call from outside and paused at the ninth step, sticking her little finger down the crack against the wall. She chuckled softly, recalling that her sister Sarah's wedding ring had been lodged in this crack for three stressful days prior to her wedding. Amanda was the ring bearer and was practising descending the long staircase with the ring perched on a little white pillow when she tripped. The ring went tumbling down the stairs and disappeared. The crack on the side of the ninth step was the perfect size for the ring and, despite the entire family looking endlessly up and down the stairs, it was not found until the day before the wedding, when Chad noticed a tiny sparkle from deep inside the crack. Sarah had not really forgiven Amanda for this debacle and the two do not exchange sisterly love very often.

The long staircase had an impressive banister. It was wide and solid and perfect for sliding down, except for the landing post. She had learned to slide rapidly down the top half, jump off at the landing, and hop on again to reach the bottom. It had been years since she had slid all the way down. The twins and Amanda had a long-running contest as to who could slide down the fastest. Being the lightest in weight and the one who could hop off and on the fastest, Amanda proudly held that record over her childhood. *One last time before I go?*

Climbing to the top, she put her leg over the wide, worn banister and headed down—only this time she slammed into the landing post. Jumping off, she acknowledged that she had lost her touch.

Sitting on the landing, Amanda recalled the many conversations she had overheard while crouched in the corner. On many occasions, she had listened to her parents laughing and teasing each other over the long years of their happy marriage. When she was eight, she learned that her granny had died by hearing her mom crying and her dad's consoling words. A week earlier, Samantha had knocked on her bedroom door and held her tight in a hug while she shared the news that granny was very sick. Amanda was not permitted to go to the hospital and say goodbye as she was too young. At that age, she didn't understand that her granny was gone forever. What upset her more were her mother's frequent tears and the loss of her mother's attention while she lived through the early stages of grief.

However, at ten, the overwhelming fear and terror over her dad's diagnosis of cancer led her to worry over how soon she might lose him, as she had her granny. She had walked up to him and told him directly that she wanted to be there when he died, that she would be there with him and no one could keep her out. Fortunately, he had recovered and was now waiting outside with her mom to drive her to the train station to start her new life at college.

Despite the quick exit she had originally planned, Amanda lingered on the landing, overwhelmed by the flood of family memories stored in the burnished oak landing.

She turned and looked up the stairs behind her, recalling that only a few months ago she was getting ready for her high school graduation prom, which was supposed to be one of the hallmarks of her life. Her best friends, Casey and Brilla, had come over to her house to get ready on the big night. They had giggled their way through the rituals of hair, nails, and make-up to become transformed into strange new beings who were almost unrecognizable even to themselves. Trying on their new heels, they took turns walking down the stairs without falling over. They pretended to be famous movie stars descending an elegant staircase to be received by their fans. As each practised carefully placing their heels down one step at a time, the other two friends stood at the bottom of the stairs whooping and hollering cheers and encouragement. Amanda's parents filmed them walking gracefully down the long staircase, recording this rite of passage to store as a permanent memory.

A half hour before Greg was supposed to arrive to pick her up, she received a text from him: "Hey meant to tell you earlier. Taking Gwyneth to prom. Sorry about that." She regretted she had already put on her mascara as her face was a mess and her black tears dripped onto her new gown, leaving little tear-shaped stains. However, for the first time, she learned what genuine friendship was, as Casey and Brilla decided to party at her house to keep her company, missing their own prom.

Chad and Curtis had left the house two years ago. Amanda thought being an only child would be ideal, having the entire house to herself. Imagine using the bathroom whenever she wanted—no more banging on the door in desperation. Imagine not having to duck as a stuffed animal or ball was thrown at her from the top of the stairs as she headed out the door. Imagine not having to beg to use the second car.

But freedom and happiness do not always mesh. She was lonely and often left the big, empty house in search of company and noise. This was not the first time she had experienced being so alone. Her life was similar to that of an only child when Chad and Curtis started elementary school, leaving her the single child at home. To compensate, she had created two imaginary friends, Golda and Silver, whom she happily played with until her brothers returned from school. When she started kindergarten, she asked her teacher if Golda and Silver could come as well.

Amanda looked up the stairs and noticed that the thirteenth step had less of a depression. She and her siblings had tried to avoid that step as much as possible, leaving step twelve with a greater indentation. This habit had stayed with her and she still avoided the number thirteen even when she was counting.

Step seven was where the cat continued to sleep, despite having its tail stomped on so many times.

Steps one and two doubled as seats to put on boots, and, in fact, had often been cluttered with boots, shoes, slippers, and schoolbooks.

But no more. She was the last child to move out of the house. The staircase would now get some well-deserved respite from the multitude of feet stampeding up and down this vertical corridor.

No longer would Amanda have to push herself to keep up with an older sibling. She was more than ready to launch. She had lived 17 years preparing for this day, transitioning to an adult much like a butterfly ready to burst out of her cozy cocoon and fly away into the unknown. What would she take with her from her childhood? As time passed would the bad memories fade and only the good ones remain? She wondered if in ten years she would still be essentially the same person. Does childhood create a fully formed adult who grows older and gets wiser, but is primarily the same person?

"Amanda, we are going to the train station without you! Get the beans out here!"

With tears in her eyes, Amanda hugged the pedestal at the bottom of the stairs and walked out, shutting the door firmly behind her.

Susan Cross/64

THE PRESENT: BLINDSIDED

It took about fifteen seconds for Jewels to capture the eyes of the cute, blond hunk throwing back his neat whiskey at the bar across the room. It was her eyelashes that cemented the connection. The all-natural, thick, jet-black lashes flowed out in the air almost up to her eyebrows like the eyelashes of a llama. His custom-fit suit and the Rolex on his wrist, combined with the super-sized diamond on his pinkie finger, satisfied the criteria upon which Jewels based her selection.

Jewels was unsure of the purpose of the event she had crashed at the Sheraton. This was an unusual state for her; she verged on the far side of the attention-to-detail spectrum. The ambience of the room revealed no clues. It clearly wasn't a wedding—most people were dressed for business, but she couldn't locate a company logo anywhere. Perhaps a family function? *I'm getting sloppy,* she thought. *Can't stub my toe at this point.*

Jewels had learned to hold tight once she threw out the first lure. Four, five minutes would pass on that Rolex before she would re-establish that binding, intense, you-could-be-the-one look. Hours of practice, first interacting with a mirror and then with her friends in random bars, had perfected the art of capturing her prey with the intensity of her eye contact. Non-verbal worked best. It was fast, the intensity lasted a New York minute, and it didn't use up too much of her time or energy.

She stood just outside the small group beside her. Two millennial couples were laughing nervously as they sipped too often on their drinks. "So, do you think he left us big bucks? Are you planning a luxurious vacation? Buying a Tesla?" More nervous laughter followed.

"Shit," Jewels accidentally said out loud. She quickly reverted to her own internal conversation. *I'm at a fucking funeral. Or maybe the reading of the will? But how could that be with so many people here?*

The brunette was dressed in a very formal business suit, creamy brown to match her eyes, bosom revealed, but in a modest way, skirt at the midline, but slit to the mid-thigh to taunt just a little. She turned to Jewels and asked, "So, what charity are you representing?"

"Um, Heart and Stroke," Jewels said, as the first charity she could think of popped into her brain, recalling the folks at the door collecting every year.

"That's a coincidence," the woman replied. "So are we. I'm Jessie; this is Rupert, our marketing manager; Lilli, our volunteer coordinator; and Kurt, our financial manager. Which branch are you with?"

Jewels unobtrusively activated her fake calls app and waited for her phone to ring. "Sorry, I have to get this, catch you later," she said as she walked away, speaking to her fake colleague. "You want me to come back to the office as soon as I can? Okay, I'll see what I can do."

Skirting the edge of the room and avoiding eye contact as much as possible, she glanced around the room, looking for her target. He was talking to an attractive blonde directly opposite her. Was she losing her touch? Did she have to pick another mark? Just then, he looked over at her and started moving her way. Jewels pushed her breasts in his direction and re-established her killer eye contact. He smiled, she waved, and they moved towards each other.

"Jeffrey, it's so great to see you again," she said as they reached each other. She gave him a warm, close hug. "Uh, my name is Pete," he said, looking confused. "Well, then you have a doppelgänger out there for sure. So sorry for the mix-up," she said as she once again activated her phone. "See you around, gotta get this," she said as she moved toward the exit.

After grabbing the next elevator up to her hotel room, she entered the room, kicked off her heels, and wiped the sweat from her brow. "I might be getting too old to pull this off anymore," she said to herself. "I won't be that cavalier again. It's too stressful."

She pulled Pete's wallet out from under her shawl. *I hope this guy's a cash dude. I hate relying on credit cards. Yeah, at least six hundred bucks. Not bad for a ten-minute stint.* Jewels had a modicum of compassion for her victims and consistently removed only cash, or one credit card if the wallet was limited to plastic, before dumping the wallet in a nearby hallway.

Jewels had been raised to expect and believe she deserved to have anything her heart desired. Over her childhood, she had quite literally been treated as the "jewel" of the family. Money flowed through the family like water. The only child of two surgeons, she spent little time with her parents, but was beloved from afar and lavished with praise, gifts, and any expensive toy she could ever want. The message came through strongly that her destiny included the best that money could buy. Although her real name was Melissa, her parents called her Jewels, and it stuck.

During her college years she looked for the perfect person to support her as an adult, but was woefully disappointed with the offerings. With minimal studying, she cruised through her courses, partied hard, drank her way through the days and nights and, fortunately, only tinkered with drugs. After college, her parents told her she had six months to figure out how to support herself. The free money came to an abrupt end.

Jewels had used her lush eyelashes to support herself through modelling for a time, but soon realized that the working world was not for her. After repeatedly studying all the YouTube videos she could find on pickpocketing, she stumbled upon a weekend pickpocketing course that was advertised as a course on "social engineering." It took her three weekends to perfect her skills. "You have the perfect hands for this work," John, the instructor, told her. Her hands were slender, her long fingers topped with elongated fingertips that curled easily around objects nestled snugly in deep pockets. Despite this advantage, she set the alarm off three times on her first practice heist. When the alarms continued to fill the room in response to her fumbling attempts over the second weekend, she realized she needed to up the ante and actually follow through with the assigned homework exercises if she were going to live the life she believed she deserved. With a sigh of relief she finished the course on the third weekend without once setting off the alarm on the dummies filled with wallets, phones, and watches.

Jewels wasn't the only person who stifled a giggle when John congratulated all the graduates and said he trusted the training would vastly improve their work as mentalists. At graduation, he had approached her to ask how she would apply what she was learning. Luckily, she had prepared herself for this question.

Jewels vowed to work only two to three days per week. This paid the rent on her luxury condo, covered the payments on her BMW convertible lease, and financed her lavish parties, with their quantities of fine wine and champagne. The older she got the more it cost to maintain the youthful look she cherished: injections, wraps, microdermabrasion, sugaring, and electrolysis weren't cheap. But it surprised even her that she was not a clothes horse; she relied on her modest collection of expensive, tailored black outfits that she could accessorize to suit the occasion.

Early in her career she concentrated on high-end bars. Intoxicated men weren't as sensitive to lingering fingers. After a few months, however, she tired of drunken breath, slurred words, and fingers fumbling for her breasts and groin. She also wanted to work during the day. A friend asked her to attend a conference on cosmetics and self-esteem, which she thought would actually be interesting. When she saw the list of companies scheduling events at the hotel she decided she was ready to graduate to luxury hotels populated with wealthy businessmen who would smell fresh and be less likely to attempt rude gestures.

Last night she had a dream that she was caught and had to do time in jail. In the morning, she laughed it off and headed out to the airport to catch a flight to Chicago. She never pickpocketed in her hometown. She told her friends that her work as a cosmetic consultant required her to travel a great deal. No one, not even her closest friends, knew how she sustained her lavish lifestyle. Only once had she run into a friend who happened to be attending the wedding function she had crashed. It was fairly easy to create the distant cousin role. She was now so used to living a life of deceit.

Jewels had booked into the Trump International Hotel. After the last fiasco, she was taking an extra day to study the event board and to thoroughly research the event. *Yes, an IT company. That's a sure thing.* To ensure all the bases were covered, Jewels reviewed the IT terminology list she had prepared for precisely this occasion. As well, she had created a fake IT persona and perfected her entrance protocol.

Planting herself outside the conference room, she watched the women entering the room to determine what to wear. Out of her three black dresses, each featuring different cleavage exposure, she would pick the one that was neither modest nor brazen. She would dress it up with long silver earrings and a silk scarf woven with silver strands of thread.

Once she was dressed suitably, Jewels joined a group of people entering the conference. "Hi," she said to the blonde replica of herself, "how's it going?" She walked over to the registration table with the group. "I'm going to hit the washroom first. See you in a bit." The blonde said, "Yeah, sure," clearly trying to place her.

As she crossed the room, walking over to the washroom, Jewels spotted her next victim. He fit the bill perfectly. She sometimes wondered if she lined them up whether she would be able to match them to the location of the heist—they all looked alike. Is that why this guy looked somewhat familiar? He was tall, with chestnut hair spiked above his forehead and shaven closely along the sides. He walked with confident posture and displayed a wide, generous smile. Jewels watched him approach the bar and order a drink. As he waited, he drummed the beat of the music on the side of his bar stool, moving slowly to the music.

Jewels positioned herself for ultimate eye contact. She garnered her sexual energy into her eyelashes and cast her spell. The eyelock buzzed across the room. It was so powerful, neither could look away. She found herself inextricably caught in the intensity of their mutual attraction. *Get a grip, girl*, she said to herself and forced herself to look away. The stimulant effect of that look jarred her. She was flushed, her breathing rapid and shallow. It threw her off balance. *I should leave right now*, she thought, but she stood still, stuck in place. At this moment, the loneliness of her life enveloped her. A serious relationship was not possible in her line of work.

However, Jewels loved a challenge. She decided to work through this disturbing feeling. This heist would take ultimate control on her part. Taking several deep breaths, she reminded herself of the many bills she had to pay, and once again searched for her intended victim.

She looked up and there he was, almost in range of speaking. "Jeffrey, it's so great to see you again," she said warmly, this time not making direct eye contact. "Melissa, it's great to see you as well," he said, giving her a long, warm hug.

Panic ran down her body as she heard her real name. The muscles in her jaw turned to steel, the saliva in her mouth was sucked dry, her brow was planted with a row of furrows. *Do your job*, she repeated silently as she reached into his pocket. Her hands were shaky as she finally slipped his wallet into her purse.

They stood apart, looking at each other with the same intense look they'd shared earlier. Jewels was tongue-tied. He also stood there in silence. At last, his phone rang. He answered and said, "Sorry, I've got to take this—hope to see you around" as he walked out of the room.

Jewels was feeling two ways about his abrupt departure. Now she had an inkling how the men she had exploited felt.

"OMG, his name really is Jeffrey," she said as she sorted through his wallet in her hotel room. "What are the odds of that?" She put on her reading glasses to look more closely at his business card. Jeffrey Stevens, MENTALIST. "What the fuck? He was in my course; no wonder he looked familiar." Opening his billfold, she found a note. "Good job. I didn't even notice you lifting it." The wallet had no credit cards or cash hidden away.

Jewels jumped out of bed and grabbed her purse. As her wallet was gone, she had lost her earnings for the day. She laid on the bed and laughed hysterically. Then she reached for her phone to congratulate him.

Susan Cross/76

THE PRESENT: Joining the Club

Phillipa looks down at her list. Dress, check—$150 on the discount rack at Holt Renfrew. She has never worn red before and feels conspicuous in such a vibrant colour. She'd chosen the colour from watching a lone cardinal in a flock of grackles at her parents' birdfeeder. Phillipa is carefully calculating exactly how to be the centre of attention.

Next on her list are shoes, which are lacking a check mark. Her feet live mostly in flip-flops, sneakers, and slippers, so she isn't used to walking in heels. During the two hours she allotted to finding shoes she'd found the perfect pair that she could walk in and that looked stylish on her somewhat wide feet. But they cost $150 and her budget is limited to $100 for shoes. She glances down at the rest of her list to see if there is something she can eliminate. She decides to ask her friend Kelly to do her mani-pedi and rushes to pick up the shoes before her hair appointment in twenty minutes.

Three hours later and $110 poorer, her hair is now highlighted with red and blonde streaks the colour of the sandstone formations she has seen in Arizona. From the hair salon, she drives directly to the mall to get the two-hour special "make-up over" at one of the department stores. Her new face is applied for free as long as she purchases a minimum of $50.00 of make-up. She picks out a $15.00 lipstick and splurges on an eyebrow and eyelash tint for $35, ticking off the last item on her list, so happy that she stuck to her $500 budget.

Arriving home, Phillipa considers the complete package, putting on her dress and shoes, sashaying as if on a fashion runway. She closes the closet door, looking critically in the full-length mirror. She sees her brown eyes widen and her full, red lips form into a surprised "O." *I'm as close to Truly Beautiful as I'll ever get; if this doesn't work, I might as well give up.*

Phillipa believes that most people can be divided into two camps: the Almost Pretty and the Truly Beautiful. Most of Phillipa's friends and Phillipa herself work hard and spend a considerable amount of money to maintain their membership in the AP Club. But tonight, Phillipa is joining the TB Club and outlining a strategy to keep her membership.

One of Phillipa's good friends, Julia, belongs to the TB Club, with almost no effort. It doesn't seem to matter what she wears or what she does, she always looks beautiful. Last week, they had hiked up Devil's Peak with the temperature soaring into the thirties. Phillipa's face had been streaked in glistening grey sweat and her shirt was sticking to her back by the time she reached the summit. Julia had worn white shorts, which were as spotless at the top as when she started out, and her sweat band had kept her hair in place and her face crisp and fresh. In fact, apart from saying she was tired from the hike, Julia looked the same.

You would think that Phillipa would resent Julia, the natural-born TB. But Julia doesn't seem to appreciate the fact that her membership in the club is sealed. In fact, being beautiful doesn't seem to be important to her, and she is generous and helpful to all her friends.

At last, it's time to go. Phillipa has been ready for two hours, amazed that she hasn't rubbed her eyes as she usually does. She practises sitting forward in a chair without resting her back to ensure her long, curly hair is not squashed. *I would fit in perfectly at Downton Abbey,* Phillipa chuckles to herself. She hasn't eaten dinner to ensure her tummy stays flat and trim.

"Hey girl," Julia says when she comes to pick up Phillipa. "You look good in red."

Phillipa's neck turns as red as her dress as she realizes how much is riding on tonight's party. Julia looks elegant in her simple white wrap dress with her hair pulled into a French knot. Phillipa starts to compare herself to Julia, but then tells herself to stop. *This is not a contest.*

As she walks into the room, she visualizes a spotlight following her. She has never been the centre of attention before, but now she feels like the cardinal, in her smart red dress. Over the last year, Phillipa has studied what she terms "the flocking effect"; pockets of people centred around a TB female. Typically she would join the sidelines of Julia's cluster, since Julia would always let her in, but tonight she is the TB female and a flock of men (and some women) vie for her attention.

Justin, who usually ignores her, moves in and puts his arm around her shoulders, steering her away from the group. "Hey, looking good, Phil," he says to her. "Liking the new look."

"You're looking not so bad yourself," Phillipa replies playfully, staring longingly into his big blue eyes. Grant, who is in her music class, joins them, saying, "Don't go off with this dude, Phillipa, he's bad company."

They all laugh and Grant sets a date for coffee after their class next week. Justin objects, saying he was there first, and asks her out for a drink next Saturday. Phillipa's eyes light up, marvelling at the fact that two men who previously would not even have noticed her are battling for her attention. Justin runs his fingers over her exposed breasts and pats her ass as he heads over to another group. Grant looks annoyed and mutters, "He's all over you and you didn't even object."

"It kinda surprised me," Phillipa says, her splotched neck again revealing her embarrassment.

Julia approaches Phillipa from across the room. "I've got such a headache, it's turning into a migraine," she says. "Can you get a ride home from someone else?" Grant overhears the conversation and says he can take Phillipa home. "Not to worry."

Phillipa walks out to the car with Julia. "I'm sorry you have to leave. This seems to happen to you quite often at parties. Perhaps it's the red wine."

Julia's face turns serious and thoughtful. "The party was great, and I was enjoying myself, but then I reach a point where I am so fed up with being hit on that I have to leave. It's been this way all my life. I don't know how many times I've had my ass pinched and my boobs squeezed by men I've barely met. I'm at the point where I cross the street if there are a group of men standing together near the sidewalk. Men always talk to me as if I were naked. It's hard to have a genuine conversation." Julia's eyes tear up and she turns away from Phillipa to hide her upset feelings.

"Really? Is that what your life is like?" Phillipa asks. "I had no idea. I have always envied you for all the attention you get."

"Well, don't," replies Julia. "It's tiring and boring. You're lucky to be free of that hassle."

Phillipa waves goodbye and turns to head back into the house. "It can't be that bad," she mutters to herself. "It seems like such a small price to pay to join the club."

Phillipa wakes up at nine a.m. with a hangover headache and mascara dripping down to the end of her nose. Even so, she curls her toes in delight and yells, "Whoopee. I made it. I think I am in!"

As she rolls over, she touches another body in the bed, facing away from her. *Oh God, this isn't my bed. Where on earth am I? Who am I with? I wonder if it's Justin or Grant. Who took me home?* Phillipa giggles to herself, guessing it is likely Grant. The giggling wakes the body up. He turns over and gazes at her. He looks neither like Justin nor Grant. In fact, she has never seen him before. "So, girl in the red dress, what was your name again?"

THE PRESENT: Planting Beds

As Dorothy's eyes crossed for the third time, she closed her eyes. The burning sensation of extreme fatigue simmered and danced across her retina like a campfire glowing with hot coals. Her right hand automatically reached for a nearby pillow embroidered with red and pink roses, which she tucked under her head seconds before she fell into a deep sleep at her desk.

The ledger lay at rest as well; no more numbers were entered into the long columns of orders taken, orders processed, invoices mailed, invoices paid. It seemed never-ending.

Dorothy's niece, Jess, snuck quietly into the house at two a.m., wondering why the lights were still on downstairs. For the second time this week she woke up her aunt and gently guided her to her bed, chastising her for once again sleeping on the job. "For Christ's sake, Aunt Dorothy, you're sixty-nine years old—you need a proper night's sleep."

"As if you can talk, young lady, staying out at all hours with that cute new boyfriend when you have to be at work at eight." Dorothy kissed her niece goodnight and gratefully lay down comfortably in her own bed to drift off once more.

In the morning, Dorothy gazed at her tired face in the mirror. New lines were etched across her face like the road map she had picked up showing the recent suburbs erupting across the city's north end. Routledge was being touted as an affordable retirement community and newly constructed housing for seniors had fostered the latest housing boom. This had caused Dorothy's business to grow exponentially, like a climbing rose fed too much fertilizer and sunshine. The business had grown too fast for Dorothy to keep up with. She felt out of control and was uncertain how to tame it into a manageable entity. She longed for the days when she and her niece managed the fledgling home business well, with orders trickling in at a slow, steady pace.

Dorothy pulled her greying hair back and clipped it up into a messy bun. She had planned to get her hair cut and styled weeks ago, but hadn't found the time. Her gym card lay in her wallet, unused for the last two months, in stark contrast to the daily exercise routine she used to maintain. Her muscles were becoming flabby, and she had gained ten pounds.

Dorothy sighed and whispered, "I only need to keep this up for a short time. It's the price you pay for being successful." She smiled to herself, recalling the comments of friends and family, telling her she was too old to start an untried business and that she would lose her retirement fund to this ridiculous idea. The orders and money were pouring in now—she simply had to keep on top of things until a more efficient system of managing the business was developed.

Baptized Dorothy Judy Garland Settler, her mother called her Dorothy or Judy interchangeably until one day Dorothy suddenly, and completely, stopped responding to Judy. She decided at a young age that she would rather be Dorothy, who was courageous enough to follow the Yellow Brick Road, rather than Judy, who was only acting and whose real life was tragic.

Dorothy grew up in a nursery, amongst seedlings, perennials, and colourful annuals. She loved talking to the baby begonias, and she created her own plant family in the begonia greenhouse, where she set up her tea set and brought her favourite stuffed animals. As an only child, the plants became her friends, and she learned how hard they worked to grow and flower in a single season.

When her parents retired from the nursery business and it was time for Dorothy to take over, the big box stores had put most of the family nurseries out of business. The profit margin was approaching zero percent, so her parents sold the business to provide a comfortable retirement for themselves.

At the age of fifty-five, Dorothy was suddenly and unexpectedly unemployed. Having never married, she had no other income to fall back on and had to search for a way to support herself. For five years she grew a market garden selling vegetables to local restaurants, supplementing her income with a stall at the city marketplace. But the long hours of heavy labour had become too much for her and she decided to try something so risky and unsettling that she needed the comfort and support of the Scarecrow, the Lion, and the Tin Man to go through with it. Against the advice of her financial planner, she cashed in all of her retirement investments and started up a new and unusual business.

It all started the day she received one of the most terrifying calls of her life. Her best friend, Jody Miller, suffered a stroke in her late fifties. Jody was fit, active, and full of life. Her stroke changed everything. Her life became small as she was confined to her home and limited to particular movements and activities. Rehabilitation was slow and uncertain.

Dorothy invited Jody to come and live with her for six months until she no longer needed daily assistance. Jody tried her best to help out, doing what she could to contribute to the household. One day, Dorothy spied Jody in the garden trying to pull weeds and pick some vegetables. "I'm part of a living system when I'm out in the garden," she said. "I feel calm and alive." However, getting up and down to tend to the plants was near agony for Jody. "I wish I could reach them more easily," she said.

In the middle of the night, Dorothy awoke with a brilliant idea. She got up at two a.m. to sketch her plan to build an upright garden—one that a person who could not easily bend down or get on their knees could easily manage. It had to be sizable enough to be a proper garden, not just a window box.

Dorothy called her friend John Stirling, who was a retired engineer. A week later, John had taken Dorothy's initial sketch and provided specifications for a well-supported upright garden bed. This was taking a raised garden bed to a new level. Dorothy ordered the materials and her nieces and nephews built the first "easy-to-tend garden bed" over a long weekend. They presented it to Jody at her birthday celebration. Through planning and tending her own garden, Jody regained purpose in her life and discovered a pleasurable activity she could do on her own.

Of course, through word of mouth, the idea spread and Dorothy started getting requests for garden beds to be made for others who had limited mobility. After the tenth order, she contacted a factory to make the beds for her and she registered her business: Upright Garden Beds.

All the early garden beds were constructed to be placed outdoors until she received an email request to build a smaller bed for indoor use. The bed was to be made for Oscar, who needed a garden bed at wheelchair height. It was back to the drawing board with John and the indoor version was created, called The Oscar.

There were now a dozen unique designs to choose from, all named after the first person who had presented different needs, given their available space and mobility. However, The Jody was still the most popular design.

As the business grew, Dorothy hired Jess, who had recently graduated with a business degree from college, to assist her. Jess had planned to move to a larger city to find a job, but was delighted to stay in Routledge and help her aunt grow her business. She had spent many summer vacations living with her aunt and loved plants and flowers almost as much as Dorothy did.

Jess was eager to contribute to the management of the business through the use of up-to-date programs that would both save time and enable the running of reports to assist in adapting to future needs. But Dorothy was resistant to streamlining her business practices. For example, she still used a paper ledger to record the orders, invoices, and payments by hand. This took hours to complete as the business grew.

Jess tried her best to convince Dorothy to modernize. "A computer can do all the calculations for you, Dorothy; we need to use technology to free up our time. Let me create a spreadsheet to show you how helpful and time-saving the computer can be."

"No, no, I likely wouldn't understand it. My system is working well."

Dorothy would not budge on this one aspect of the business and Jess had given up trying to persuade her. As the weeks passed, Dorothy was reluctant to admit to Jess that the business was suffering from the bookkeeping backlog, with three weeks of orders and invoices waiting untouched.

She paused as the familiar signs of anxiety took over her body, starting in her stomach and working its way to the slight tremble in her right hand. If only she could lie down and rest, but that was not an option. For the next two hours, she furiously entered number after number in the ledger and at least got the new orders recorded.

"I've finished calling everyone who had placed an order on the sheets you gave me, Dorothy. Are the orders finally slowing down?" Jess said with a sigh of relief as she came into the small office and gave Dorothy a kiss on the head. That small, kind gesture was the breaking point for Dorothy who broke down, sobbing into her hands. "I'm so far behind, Jess—I can't keep up anymore; maybe this is too much for me."

Jess sat down, cupping Dorothy's hands in hers. "I've noticed how tired you've become, how late at night you are up working with these figures, and I wondered why I have no more orders to call. Please let me design a bookkeeping system that will speed things up, Dorothy. I honestly can do it. You lie down for a couple of hours and once you're up, I'll make you a cup of sweet tea."

As Dorothy lay quietly in her room, she fretted over how to rescue the business. What a fool she had been to hoard the financial end of the business to herself when Jess had the training to make the running of the business more efficient. *You stupid fool—so stubborn and independent. I wonder if I've left it too late, if we can catch up.*

As Dorothy got out of bed to get back to work, her balance failed her, and she had a debilitating headache. She cried out for help, but Jess didn't hear her. She lay back in bed, afraid to move. *I'll try falling asleep and see if that helps me feel better*, she thought; but she didn't sleep. She lay there in fear and dread.

When Jess brought her a cup of tea a few hours later, she realized Dorothy needed an ambulance immediately. "Why didn't you call me?" she said as tears rolled down her face. But Dorothy couldn't speak clearly; she was just grateful that Jess had come at last.

In the hospital, Dorothy finally had all the time in the world to rest. But resting wasn't what she wanted. She longed to be involved in the business, even in some small way. As her speech gradually returned, she decided to use her knowledge of the plant world to advance their sales. Dorothy spent many hours in the outdoor patio of her hospital wing designing fully planted beds; from all-vege beds, to flowering beds, and one that embraced companion planting. Dorothy was in her element. Clearly, conceiving new garden beds along with her expertise on adapting plant materials to best fit the needs of the buyer were her strengths. She vowed to leave Jess fully in charge of the administrative and financial end of the business.

When Dorothy returned home from the rehabilitation hospital, she found a brand new model of a garden bed in the family room—in fact, it took up most of the room and was built like a small maze so that she could wander around at will. The Dorothy was the largest and most complex of all the designs built for people who really did follow the Yellow Brick Road.

THE PRESENT: Tra La 123

It's times like this that I am unsure if I am insane. I feel completely normal. Looking around at my surroundings, I suspect there must be something still wrong with me. But if there really is something wrong with me, why wouldn't I have an inkling, just an inkling?—which I do not. I have, in fact, felt uninsane for quite some time now.

So, I have been planning my escape. I do not believe if I asked to leave the door would open. I'm not so stupid as to fall into that trap. Watching heist movies and TV shows has helped me design the details of my escape. For example, on *White Collar*, Neil escapes from prison in daylight by transforming his appearance and wearing a guard's uniform. He actually walks out of prison in broad daylight. I know, I know; —it's just a TV show. But don't you think it's not such a bad idea?

My prison has nurses rather than guards, but the purpose is the same: to keep us in hell and away from the rest of the world. As a woman, it is harder to change my appearance because of my lack of facial hair. I am, however, gradually changing my looks to make the great escape easier to achieve. My hair now hangs down to my shoulder blades and my eyebrows have grown rather bushy, which I detest, and find I can't look at myself in the mirror anymore. Quick glances are allowed to ensure I don't have any food stuck to my chin or entwined in my hair, but I don't look myself in the eye. I have stuffed my bra and underpants with padding, gradually looking fatter. In fact, they changed my diet the other day, and I was starving! I even stole a hellmate's glasses last week and laid them in my junk drawer, right out in the open as if they were a pair of glasses I no longer use. I'm getting quite fond of this concept of deception, Hidden in Plain View. It keeps me amused.

When you say Tra La 123, you need to give each of the three parts their own beat, so Tra and La are said with one beat each and then you need to fit all the numbers 123 in the third beat. This comes from a skipping game I used to play when I lived in England as a child. Using two long ropes, the two girls twirling the ropes swing one rope for two beats, and then, on the third beat, the rope comes from the other direction. The skipper has to be ready for that—an onslaught from another direction like a boomerang or a barb thrown from nowhere in the middle of an argument. But all the skipper needs to do is jump and make sure there is space between her feet and the ground. It doesn't, in fact, matter from which direction the rope comes; what matters is that the skipper has the will and concentration to ensure that space is there, the space that ensures the rope will go by smoothly and she has survived to prepare for the next round.

I'm sitting in the lounge with the big windows looking out over the acres of grass—no one wants to live too close to us. I kind of miss the squeaking sound of the pee-proofing plastic the cushions used to be wrapped in. I guess they now trust us to use the bathroom like normals do. Take a look at those two over in front of the window. No, not the two men sitting staring out into space with their vacant, medicated eyes. A little more to the left and you'll see Mr. and Mrs. Carrier—Eddie and Urma. Imagine, they're in here together. I often wonder what their story is. Did they drive each other crazy? Did they live in an environmental hazard zone that slowly ate up their brains? What would happen if one of them gets discharged, and the other has to stay? Would the sane one leave?

Oh, here comes Dr. McNather. Quick, put on a plastic smile (check); keep eye contact (check); make a cheery comment (check). Every day, for the last six months, I have purposefully performed ten normal, noticeable acts a day (I prefer to call them "acts" because I really am acting). I smile, I engage in meaningless small talk, I paint little pictures of tranquil scenes and I tend my own small garden patch. I am a model patient. It is only at night that I allow myself to feel real. I scream silently into my pillow. I let a tear or two run down my face—I like the taste of the salt.

The only meds I swallow are my anti-psychotics. I have finally realized that no one, not even me, likes me without them. The major hole in my escape plan is how I would get them on the outside. Maybe I can get them on the street. I can't exactly sign up with a family doc and ask for them.

The escape date is set for two weeks from today. My stomach quivers when I say that to myself. I've arranged with Harold, who got out on the legit a few months ago, to stay with him until I can figure out what to do. Will Harold want sex for payment? Yeah, probably, but hey, I haven't had any in a very long time.

You're wondering why I'm not heading home to my family? You wouldn't wonder if you'd seen how I've alienated everyone who has tried to give me a chance. Cinders, I say—burnt those bridges to cinders. Can't be helped now.

What would it be like to walk down the street, the wind in my hair, the sun on my face, the birds singing in my ear? No one watching me; no one assessing my saneness. What would it be like to go into a grocery store and pick out food I actually like, to be cooked by me? I can't wait to try out living a boring normal life. No more plastic smiles; no more white, monotonous corridors; no more pills of every shape and colour.

Okay, another day of time served has passed. Tomorrow I have an appointment with Dr. McNather for my semi-annual assessment. What questions will she ask this time? What year is it? Who is the prime minister? (Jeez, who wants to even think about that?) What is my mother's maiden name? I'm ready for this—five deep breaths before I go in. Although, in actuality, I don't even need to pass this one, as I'm outta here in two weeks anyway.

Although I wake up at dawn (not my usual stint), I slept well. I feel refreshed and ready for the day. This might be a good day for me. They even had waffles for breakfast with fresh strawberries. What a treat.

I arrive at Dr. McNather's office fifteen minutes early to show I am interested and punctual. As I walk into her office, I remark on a new picture hung above the sofa. It is a beautiful pastoral scene of a field dotted with colourful wild flowers. How I would love to walk barefoot through the field. They discourage bare feet when walking outdoors here for obvious reasons.

Dr. McNather is a fine psychiatrist. She doesn't probe too deeply and treats you like a human being. Although her voice tone is warm, she doesn't have that fake caring voice that many staff here use.

"So, Josie, we've noticed a spectacular improvement in your behaviour and attitude over the last six months. Your medications are now stabilized, and you have met all our requirements for a gradual discharge from this ward. We want to talk to you today about where you can live, starting at two days a week with support beginning as soon as next week. What do you think? Would that work for you?"

My head is clouding up, my eyes are frozen in fear, my limbs are fully contracted. I don't know where to look. *Keep those thoughts buried—don't let them out. Oh no, they're getting out. What am I saying? What am I doing?* My hidden self has taken over; I try one last time to stuff her down where she belongs, but I don't have a hope. I try to keep skipping. I try to keep the space there, just under my feet, but the rope comes thundering down, and I lay splayed on the concrete.

THE PRESENT: Living at One

A mournful wail flows out of Gloria's mouth. It circles the furniture in the living room, dispersing the dustballs under the couch; it then floats out into the kitchen and heads up the stairs. About halfway up the stairs, it stops and dissipates, settling to the floor. The startling silence that follows is almost more alarming than the desolate cry.

Gloria's face is empty of emotion. Her eyes are vacant and unfocused. Her mouth is open, forming a small "o." (If someone else had been in the living room and seen the stunned look on her face, that person would have difficulty identifying the sentiment Gloria was feeling.)

Gloria is lying on the newly installed carpet in her living room. On the toe of her slipper sits a gob of poo. The dirty diaper she slipped on landed in the middle of her two legs, which are splayed far apart as she tries to avoid the excrement spread out over the carpet like peanut butter on toast.

She continues to lie still as her back is throbbing, and she is afraid to move in case it gets worse. Tears dribble down the side of her face onto the new carpet, but the condition of the carpet is no longer a priority for her. She just wants her old life back.

Gloria hears a car door shut and realizes she needs to move. She drags herself to a sitting position and gently pushes herself into a standing position. "Okay, not so bad," she mutters as she scurries to the bathroom to wash the signs of sadness off her face.

"We're home," Ashley calls out as she slams the front door, carrying baby Jeffrey in the car seat in one hand and a bag of groceries in the other. Gloria takes Jeffrey and unbundles him from the seat and his snowsuit. He giggles and squeals as Gloria plays with his tiny fingers and toes. She becomes human again as she holds him to her heart.

Taking a deep breath, Gloria says, "You left a dirty diaper on the carpet in the living room. I slipped on it and fell and now there is poo on the new carpet."

"I wondered why you would get a new carpet when you knew there was a baby moving in," Ashley replies. "I hope it comes out okay," she says as she picks up the bag of groceries and disappears into the kitchen.

Gloria's oldest daughter, Crystal, climbs the stairs from the basement bedroom, still in her PJs., along with Chatty, the out-of-control, barky dog she brought with her when she moved back home two months ago. Chatty runs into the living room, grabs the diaper in his teeth and shakes it back and forth, spraying you-know-what all over the carpet as he scampers around the room.

Gloria reverts to her stunned pose, unable to utter a word or, indeed, to respond at all. Crystal runs after Chatty, yelling "bad doggie, bad doggie." She finally nabs the dog and disposes of the dirty diaper. Looking at the shock on her mom's face, she thinks to herself that this may be the last straw—she could end up right back on the street.

Without uttering a word, Gloria walks slowly and carefully to her bedroom, firmly shuts the door, darkens the room and lies on the bed, feeling empty.

Crystal walks into the kitchen and rips into her younger sister. "Why the fuck would you leave a dirty diaper on the new carpet? How are we going to get it clean?"

Ashley looks at her with disdain. "You have no idea how hard it is to look after a baby, especially living with our parents. You certainly never offer to help. And why would you bring that revolting dog with you? It creates more problems than Jeffrey does."

"Right now, Chatty is all I have. How can you be so cold and heartless?" Crystal yells as she grabs the dog and heads back down to the basement, slamming the door.

Gloria gets up and throws on her running gear. She sticks ten bucks in her pocket along with her house keys and slips out the back door. As she runs along the path that surrounds the small lake near their house, her emotions surface, one by one. First, intense anger at both her daughters and the fates that brought them both home at the same time. Next, fear over how long they both might stay; this could go on for months. Then, a profound sense of relief that she could provide a home for them when their lives were upended. Finally, an overwhelming feeling of sadness at how hopeless it all seems.

She finishes her run and walks to Great Coffee: -Great Company for her morning latte.

"Hey, Glory—showing off again in your running gear?" Daniel, a good friend and neighbour, says as he comes to join her at her table. Gloria bursts into tears without saying a word.

"What's wrong, Glory?" he asks. "Has something awful happened?" Daniel's face turns red with embarrassment and he clearly wishes he were somewhere else.

"It's my kids living at home, Daniel. It's a disaster—every day seems to get worse. I now try to avoid being in my own home. I'm not sure what to do."

Daniel shakes his head, "I know, it must be difficult. I can't imagine having a baby in the house again."

"The only good thing about this arrangement *is* the baby. It's my own kids who are driving me crazy." Gloria wipes the tears from her eyes. "Thanks for listening."

"I'll get Jane to call you," Greg says as he puts on his jacket and heads for the door. "Gotta get to work. See you soon."

Gloria grabs another coffee, takes three deep breaths and sits down to think. She has tried establishing rules; those last about a day. Maybe she and John could move to the cottage, but it isn't adequately winterized and would be so cold, and she would feel isolated there. No, she needs to figure out how she is going to survive this period of her life. She tries to focus on the fact that it won't last forever.

"If happiness can be measured on a scale from zero to five, where zero is 'utter unhappiness'; one is 'just getting by — –I'm not happy or unhappy, I just am'; three is 'being happy at least fifty per cent of the time'; and five is 'deliriously happy,' perhaps I could lower my expectations and try living at one for now while the kids are at home."

What would living at one be like?

Gloria goes to the washroom and tries putting on a five face. Her face looks vibrant, excited and focused. Her skin is pink and shiny. She has colour in her cheeks. Her obvious fives were her wedding day and the birth of her two children. But she recalls that publishing her first poem and saving a child's life at the cottage also warranted a five. Happily, she realizes she has had a smattering of fives over her lifetime.

A three face is much easier for her. Her eyes show some interest and concern. Her smile is genuine, but not elated. Her attention is focused, but not intense. She suddenly realizes that much of her life has been lived at three—well, she would say between three and four. This would represent an average day of tasks and responsibilities, some not so exciting, such as cleaning the house, others that were perks along the way, such as having friends over for a meal or reading a good book.

Finally, she tries a one face. Looking in the mirror, she sees her eyes look calm, but have little sparkle and interest; her smile is subtle and somewhat mysterious. She notices she looks fairly relaxed and the wrinkles around her eyes and mouth have mellowed. Surprisingly, she doesn't appear nearly as tense as she has over the past few days. In fact, she feels little joy, but also little sorrow.

Living at one with the odd day of two or three is what she decides to try. A one face can easily handle a new carpet covered in poo.

THE FUTURE: To Stay or To Go?

Katie squats on the beach, her soles flat on the sand, her knees akimbo and sticking up to the sky. Her knees are browner than the rest of her legs from holding this pose. When she needs to reflect on a challenging situation she reverts to squatting and focusing inward. It is a pose she has used frequently in the past month. Being able to squat with her feet flat on the ground is one of those small things that makes Katie proud. Before she started using the pose for mindful meditation she used to glance around, trying to see if anyone was impressed with her perfect squat.

She picks up a branch and sweeps away any lingering pebbles. A wave rolls up and mixes with the sand, pushing a small pink crab into the cleared space. The crab darts under a rock, leaving the area clear again. She can feel the sand and water ooze between her toes and as she watches the water recede, she focuses on keeping her balance. The bubbles leave a thin layer of white foam on the sand like the lacy doily on her Nana's side table.

Before the next wave can wash away her work, Katie scratches the biggest question mark she can in the allotted space. She digs the period below the large curve with the end of the branch, creating a gaping hole in the sand. Her future feels similar to this gaping hole. A wave suddenly washes her question mark away. She repeats the pattern three times as waves continue to erase her work. If only her decision were this easy.

Katie loves to take moments like these and freeze them in her memory. In this instant, she is shielded from the major decision she has yet to make. Sometimes she wishes she could be a statue, frozen into this pose forever. What would the artist name this statue of a young woman carving out a question mark in the sand? Not *The Thinker*, that was taken. What about *The Deliberator or The Contemplator?* She ponders whether she has the body an artist could use as a model for this sculpture. Are her legs the right length, her hair the right texture?

Katie slowly releases her pose, stands upright and stretches, splaying her toes as far as they can go to make as much contact with the sand as possible, steadying her as a bigger wave tries to destabilize her. Walking over to her bicycle, she mounts and decides to take the longer route to Starbucks. Slowly Katie wends her way along the bicycle path, people-watching as she goes. She notices a large family picnicking together and tears come to her eyes. Her family means so much to her. How can she say goodbye to her mom, in whom she can confide almost anything? And to her little sister, Willa, who at 14 is much more rebellious than she had been? Raising Willa alone won't be easy for her mom. Katie is at a turning point in her life and the optimal path to take is unclear. At 22, should she make decisions based on her future or prioritize her family?

Choosing her favourite route downtown, she follows the shoreline, looking carefully at each passing scene, and wonders what her life would be like without this familiar path as part of her life. She secretly says goodbye to the pink cobblestones as her bike rat-a-tats over them; to Angler's Bay, currently packed with boats docked in the busy downtown area; to Muddy Waters, her favourite pub/bistro. It's these precious details that are hard to give up.

At Starbucks, she meets her BFF Stella, who has already ordered their capps and is sitting at a table outside. Stella waves her over, giving her a hug and a quick kiss on the cheek.

Her curly red hair bounces as she excitedly greets her good friend. "So, tell me, have you decided?" she asks with a serious look on her face. "I think so," Katie responds grimly.

* * * * *

Jack is sorting through his apartment, trying to decide what to throw out, give away, or pack and take with him. One picture of his family is likely enough. The others he can gift to his sister, Lisa. He has lots stored on his computer, anyway. Should he bring his baseball glove or his football? It's expensive to ship to South Africa, so he needs to be thoughtful about this even though the company is paying. He tosses them into the shipping pile.

Glancing out the window at the park across the street, Jack realizes he will be out of this town in two weeks. He can't wait. Lately, he has been feeling stagnant and stuck, that his life has become boring and routine. *I'm ready for fresh adventures and new people in my life.* His company transferring him to South Africa was akin to finding gold at the end of the rainbow. The thought of moving to Africa is exhilarating, just the change he knows will allow him to grow and flourish.

As he pulls storage items from under his bed he stumbles upon Buster the Bear, his good friend from childhood. "Why did I keep this dirty thing all these years?" he mumbles as he throws the stuffed animal onto the discard pile. Most of the memorabilia under the bed has been deposited in the garbage. "A clean slate," he says proudly. "I'm starting fresh."

He glances at his watch. In half an hour, he will meet Katie to discuss the final arrangements for their move. He hopes she is as excited as he is.

* * * * *

"Listen, you've made the right decision," Stella says to Katie as she gives her a panda hug. "I know it's been difficult, but you've considered all the pros and cons; you need to live with your choice. Phone me any time, you know I'm here for you."

"You are my rock, you know that. Thanks so much for your support. Love you."

Katie unlocks her bike feeling settled now; she's ready to tell Jack her decision. She wants to do it in person.

Katie cycles steadily along Credit Avenue, the shortest route to Jack's apartment, although the busiest as well. She'd prefer to continue along the water's edge, but that would take half an hour longer. After all, she is eager to share her decision.

A few blocks from Jack's house, Katie smells smoke and pulls over to the side of the road as a fire engine roars by, sirens blaring. Katie knows she should phone Jack and cycle away from the fire, but right now, the sensible Katie is not in charge. With fear adding extra energy to her physical self, she bursts out from the curb without turning to look for oncoming traffic.

Katie feels the impact on her left leg as she is hurled into the air, landing on the windshield of the blue Toyota Corolla and shattering it into a million pieces before bouncing off onto the pavement below. She gazes at the protruding bone in her leg, trying to identify this unfamiliar object. What the hell has happened?

Hours later, lying on a hospital bed in a hallway of the busy ER, Katie reflects on who it was she chose to call when asked by the paramedics whom they should notify of her accident. Surprisingly, it wasn't Jack. This would be the logical time to call him, she knows, but cell phones are prohibited near medical equipment. Hopefully, her mom has called Jack. He must be so worried she didn't show up at the scheduled time.

* * * * *

Jack wonders if Katie has been delayed. She should have been here by now. He knows she is fraught with uncertainty about whether to move to South Africa with him. Leaving her family is a much bigger deal for her, and he tries to be patient with her indecision. Their three years of, first, friendship and then intimacy should tip her decision to come with him, he thinks. She needs to break free of this town as well.

He is not all that close to his family, having left home at seventeen. Jack is one of six siblings, and it was a constant struggle for his parents to feed and clothe everyone. As the oldest of the horde Jack grew up quickly, with adult responsibilities thrust on him at a young age. It was a relief to focus on his own life, to make decisions that ensured he would not live in poverty, but he was always fighting that recurrent fear of never having enough. His salary increase should cut a major chunk out of the large student debt he acquired in obtaining his mining engineering degree.

Jack hopes and prays Katie will accompany him. He doesn't want to text her, to hound her; after all, she is only fifteen minutes late.

The discard pile is a clear winner in size compared with the recycle/give away heap of items too decent to throw away. Surprisingly, the stack of clothing and personal items to be transported to his new life is the smallest of the three. Each item has been painstakingly selected. Of course, his gravel bike has to accompany him. It took months of research to find the perfect bike to fit his six-foot-three-inch frame. He can't wait to tackle the mountain bike trails in South Africa. Katie's face lit up when he showed her the Attakwas Extreme, a killer mountain bike route through tough terrain. He had already decided to sign up for the full Attakwas Extreme route of 121 kilometres. Katie had already chosen the Attakwas Half.

The move needs to signal a new life; too many reminders of his old life will stymie his sense of adventure and curtail new opportunities. Jack can't believe how much junk he has collected over the past three years. Putting on his earphones, he turns up the music, blaring Metallica into the airwaves, filling his body with the powerful rhythm that makes him feel vibrant and alive.

He doesn't know why he didn't smell the smoke. He knows why he didn't hear the fire alarm.

Finally, his brain pulls together all the signs that his apartment building is on fire: his watery eyes, the smoke seeping under the door, the acrid taste in his mouth. Jack forces down a moment of panic. *I need to stay calm.* He remembers to stay low on the ground and crawls to the door. The doorknob is hot. *Should I open the door or stay inside?* "Stay put, stay put," he says out loud to reassure himself that this is the most sensible decision. Jack crawls to the bathroom, wets a large bath towel and lays it along the bottom of the door. He uses his packing tape to seal the door as much as possible.

Should I go out on the balcony? No, not a good plan. *But how will the fire fighters know I am here?*

His ability to think clearly is diminishing, and it is more difficult to breathe. He starts to cough and covers his mouth with another wet towel. Hearing the fire engines arrive, Jack stands at his balcony window, waving frantically. But he can't catch his breath and coughing overtakes him as he falls to the floor, hoping against hope that they will find him alive.

THE FUTURE: Limited Letters

"Oh crap, I'm out of Gs again. This is the second time this month I've had to buy more."

"What do you expect with a name like Georgina Guggenheim? You're well aware you're supposed to input your citizen number anyway."

"Yeah, so how often do you use up your letters, with a name like Nate Smith? You hardly dispose of any letters at all with that name."

Georgina flipped yet another Keurig espresso pod into the machine and waited for the melty liquid to fill her cup. She needed it this morning.

"Aren't you sick to death of limiting your communications to ten tweets per day?" she asked. "Remember the days when we used email and could write as many letters as we wanted?"

"Well, limiting our letters makes us pause and carefully contemplate what we're going to write and who we're going to contact. Consider yourself lucky. As academics, we receive double the number of letters every month and can transmit double the number of tweets."

Georgina frowned. "My sleep suffered last night as I was fixated on the book club that recently got busted in Boston. They were one of the groups we swapped books with. It's getting more and more difficult to hide them. We carry ours in diaper bags with a spray can of coyote urine in case we need to disguise our cargo. I miss my books so much." Georgina's face puckered as a sob slipped from her lips. "I'm feeling so down."

Nate walked across the office and put his hand on her shoulder. "Listen, Georgie, I know I've said this before, but you ought to let the past go and live in the present. It doesn't help to mourn the old ways. Ever since Ivanka shattered the glass ceiling by becoming president following Trump's second term in office, you've been in a major slump. I'm worried about you continuing with that book club. You could lose your job over it."

"So, you can effortlessly shed the past and embrace the new regulations? A fucking limit on the number of letters we can use to express our thoughts, a fucking limit on the number of communications we are allowed to send, a fucking limit on the length of our communications and the time they can be saved—everything we write disappears after one week. How can you call yourself a philosophy professor and support this? Our mission is to examine the hard questions of life—you can't do that in a tweet."

Nate returned to his seat and sat quietly in thought. "You realize there is a rationale for what the government is doing. The internet had imploded with information. It was on the verge of collapsing completely unless strict rules were established. Isn't it preferable for people to think clearly and thoughtfully about what they are sharing online? The Slow Thought movement is a positive change, from my perspective."

"Jesus, Nate—you're one of them! I had no idea you supported this infringement of our rights. What philosophical movement do you belong to now—the Slow Thought/No Thought movement? Doesn't it drive you crazy that we are limited to assigning our students 2,500 words a week to read? The brain needs freedom to think freely."

"How can I say this kindly, Georgie? You've fallen behind. We live in a new world and it's time to adapt. Your in-depth exploration of topics and use of so much time, conversation, and letters doesn't reflect the present reality. We've embraced a minimalist approach to the use of words and thoughts. It helps us to be clear and concise."

"Not only is that unkind, Nate, it's ridiculous. I didn't realize our world views overlap so little. As we share an office, we ought to be civil to each other, so let's leave it at that."

Nate glared at Georgina. "Well, I tried. Good luck with your fossilized thinking."

Georgina glanced at Nate to ensure he wasn't looking before she moved the materials for her upcoming seminar from her locked desk drawer into her briefcase. It was an ongoing struggle to teach Morality in Modern Society because of the hypocritical content she was forced to include. She had only occasionally dipped into the morass of immoral policies and decisions owned and operated by the current government. When she had alluded to the constraints created by the Slow Thought movement, the class response was hushed and minimal. No one, including herself, could protest too loudly. The consequences of protest inevitably led to the downright sacrifice of a decent-paying job and social status. Look what happened to her nephew, Gord, last year. His personal protest involved simply reading a book during his lunch hour, sitting on a park bench while eating his lunch. He did this for a week. No one ever talked to him about the incident. Then, one day, he noticed the book had disappeared from his desk at work and, soon after, fake news reports surfaced on social media that he watched child pornography. He was fired from his job and, one year later, was still searching for a position.

Georgina took a brave breath. It may have been the bravest breath she had ever taken. It was her turn to rock the boat. Significant leaks had sprung from her tightly wound rage. She regretted she had not run this idea by her partner, Franny. Franny was so sensible and over the years had reined in some of Georgina's more foolish attempts to change the world. To calm her inner trembling, she chuckled as she recalled the time Franny stopped her from writing Women Bleed in red paint on the women's washroom doors when the university stopped providing feminine hygiene products in the washrooms. She had limited her protest to writing a letter in red ink to the dean of women, a lashing out that led nowhere.

Georgina walked into the classroom. There were only twelve students in this class, a fourth-year seminar. She considered these students to be the brightest and most socially aware of the current cohort. She had decided to risk it all.

"Good morning, everyone. Today we are delving into entirely new subject matter. The study of this material would most certainly not be condoned by the current administration of this university. If you do not want to be implicated in sharing contentious information, I invite you to leave the room. It will not affect your mark, nor my opinion of you as a student. I am introducing more pertinent material within this course that attempts to analyze morality in the world in which we live. This work will not be described in the syllabus, nor will you be tested on it. In fact, I am asking you not to share our discussions over the next four weeks outside this class. If you decide to stay, I will ask you to sign a confidentiality agreement, binding you to discuss this material solely in this room. I can't tell you more before asking you to make your decision. Please exit now if you believe this unexpected turn is not for you."

Stan and Jean stood up and waved goodbye to the group. "We are heading into law school next year and this sounds too risky for us," Stan said as he took Jean's hand and departed, closing the door behind them.

After the confidentiality agreements were signed and collected, Georgina opened her briefcase and distributed ten books to the students. Leslie hyperventilated. Her face turned bright red and her eyes darted around the room, trying not to look at the book. Georgina handed her a paper bag.

"Anyone else need to breathe deeply to calm down? You can leave now if you wish, but remember that you have signed a confidentiality agreement." To Georgina's surprise, nobody left; however, Leslie's hands were still trembling, and she had not picked up the book.

"As you know, Bill 1101 sets out the restrictions concerning the number of words and letters we can use in written communication, and the length of articles that can be read and created. Clearly, an entire book is against the rules. I consider you to be intelligent, creative people who should be allowed to conduct an in-depth analysis using all the resources that ought to be available to you. We will read this book in class. There is a Do Not Disturb: Testing in Progress sign on the classroom door. I will collect all the books at the end of class and distribute them again each week to minimize your individual risk. Should I be caught, you will be advised that our seminar is cancelled, but no one will know that you were reading a book. Are you ready to start?"

Georgina glanced around the room. The students appeared to be in frozen animation. They sat stock-still, uncertain grimaces on their faces. Georgina's face clouded over with worry and confusion. Finally, Bart called out in glee, "Let's get to it. This is our chance to actually read a book." Everyone except Leslie joined in the conversation and excitement. Sarah prodded Leslie, saying, "It's not going to bite you—go ahead."

Leslie stood up, walked to the door, and then returned to her seat.

Eyes lit up as students gingerly picked up their copy of *Lord of the Flies*. "Today, let's read the first chapter and chat about it once everyone has finished reading," Georgina said. "Don't take any notes that leave this room."

"The fact that they picked Ralph as the leader for his good looks and affable character is so wrong," Charlotte said as the discussion began. "You get a sense right from the beginning that the boys are picking the wrong guy."

"Piggy clearly is the smart one, but the others will never follow him. Why do most people fawn over leaders who act like movie stars?" Leslie volunteered in a quiet voice. The other class members nodded their heads and smiled back at her to acknowledge her contribution.

A lively discussion ensued, focusing on the moral obligations of a democratic leader. "Can only history provide the measure of a moral leader?" Bart asked. "Are we able to step back and assess our own times?"

"Why do I feel so guilty even discussing these questions?" Leslie asked. Carol and Jason agreed, saying they felt nauseous from talking so honestly. "So this is what it is like to safely say what is on your mind," Bart replied. "It's unreal."

Georgina gathered up the books at the conclusion of class, feeling a combination of tranquility and elation that had long been missing from her everyday life.

"I've finally taken the step I needed to live like an authentic person again," she said to Franny on the phone as she asked her to meet her for a drink at The Bar.

"Oh dear, I wonder what you have got yourself into?" Franny responded. "I'll see you there."

Over the next two weeks, the classes became more animated and intense. Students were challenging each other's opinions and relating the material to philosophical theories.

In week three, a cleaner opened the door and entered the room. The sudden silence was startling. "I heard loud noises coming from a classroom with a sign that says testing is in progress," the woman said. "I thought perhaps some students were having a party and messing up the room."

Georgina rushed over to the cleaner to block her sight of the books on the desks. "This is a group oral exam," she explained. "I'm marking the students on their debating skills."

"Oh, that explains it then," the cleaner said. "It looks as if you will do this over several weeks?"

"Only one more week. Don't be concerned about the noise." Georgina breathed a sigh of relief as the woman left the room.

"Just one more? Couldn't we continue?" Bart asked.

"We need to carefully weigh the risk," Georgina replied, rubbing her forehead. "Perhaps we could meet at my house. However, next week should be our last in such a public place."

At dinner that night, Georgina raised her glass of red wine with a broad smile on her face. "I feel reborn, Franny. I have truly made a difference to these young minds." They clinked their glasses in a celebratory toast.

"I honestly thought this would turn out badly for you," Franny said. "I'm so glad it's worked out; but also relieved it's ending."

Georgina had not mentioned the possible continuance of the class in their house.

In the morning, Georgina received a summons to the dean's office. She read the anonymous tweet that had been sent to the dean: "Anyone peeked into Georgina Guggenheim's Morality and Modern Society classroom recently? In fact, you are invited not to do so, with the Do Not Disturb—Testing in Progress sign on the door. How long does this testing go on?

Why is there such a lively discussion happening? Come on, Georgina, what is really happening in that classroom?"

Georgina's insides shifted abruptly, from calm contentment to throbbing near-hysteria. Bile crept up into her mouth, bringing an acrid taste that fully embodied her panicked reaction. Who had betrayed her? What would happen to her students? She retreated to her office to sort out her thoughts and plan a strategy. She sat at her desk in a daze, breathing in and out in loud gasps of breath.

The door opened, and Nate entered the office. He walked straight to his desk without a glance over at Georgina. Neither said a word. Finally, without turning around and looking at Georgina, Nate choked out a few words. "What right do you have to put my niece, Leslie, at risk? Ruin your own life, but leave the students' alone."

"How did you know? Did you send the tweet to the dean?"

"Leslie told me about the amazing class you were teaching. I wanted to find out why she was so enthralled, so yesterday I stood outside the classroom, fascinated by the intense discussion and debate happening inside. I opened the door and peeked inside and saw the books. Everyone was so engaged; no one noticed me. I was so torn. On the one hand,

I've never seen students so involved in learning, but on the other hand, I couldn't believe you would resort to risking the future lives of your students. Yes, I'm the person who tweeted the dean—I used my last precious tweet of the month."

Georgina quickly tweeted that next week's class was cancelled. Slowly she packed up her personal belongings before heading to the dean's office, wondering how she would break the news to Franny.

THE FUTURE: Space Suit Soccer

Jeremiah had never run outdoors in his PSS (Personal Space Suit) before. In fact, it was discouraged by the government. Rule #1 for space suit use was to stay calm to limit the amount of coolant you consumed while outside in the arid, searing hot atmosphere of the planet. A slow walk, gently swinging your arms was recommended.

But today was an unusual day, an exceptional day. Jeremiah and his friends had received special dispensation from the local authority to play the game of football or soccer for thirty minutes in their PSSs. The directors had not yet decided whether to call the game football or soccer; it was a complicated decision. This event was being streamed live as part of the Sports Revival series, an initiative that sought to revive team sports from the past. To date, basketball and cricket matches had been introduced, but these competitions had been played only indoors. This was the inaugural demonstration of a team sport outdoors.

In the 25th century, team sports had vanished. Climate conditions had worsened to such an extent that it was mandated people spend only fifteen minutes each day outside without the protection of a space suit. The sun was so intense that several layers were required, even for those precious few minutes. Everyone was encouraged, however, to go outdoors daily to benefit from the stimulation of the senses that only the natural world could provide. Boardwalk paths wandered through scrub desert plants consisting primarily of gnarled, woody brush and an assortment of cacti that at times surprised the visitor with their vivid colours of purples and pinks in the spring months. Many people stretched their fifteen minutes to thirty, especially in April, when the colours were at their peak, but that was also when hospitals created special burn units for those who extended their time too far.

A football/soccer field had been created by laying Astro Turf over sand, which had been flattened by rolling the sand repeatedly by machine. Although the turf remained somewhat softer than ideal, Jeremiah was pleased it worked so well.

As captain of his team, Jeremiah felt an inordinate pride in this premier event. After extensive research, they chose

Manchester United as their team's name and recreated the team's old emblem featuring the famous Red Devil in the centre of their logo. Their competing team had chosen a modern theme instead, calling themselves the Gamma Rays.

The teams had practised only indoors, wearing their PSSs, to ensure they fully understood the rules and plays involved and to practise getting up off the ground when they fell. The pressurized cool air circulating through the space suit made it soft and pliable, and standing up in it was rather like trying to raise yourself from the ground wrapped in a thick comforter. Consensus was reached with both teams agreeing to modify a few of the rules. Having a teammate extend a hand to pull up a fallen member was agreed to by all.

The coin toss had been done indoors, with the Gamma Rays winning. Jeremiah quivered in excitement as the first kick-off commenced, with the ball flying high and deep into their end. Lucy Endermyer blocked the ball with her chest and bounced it over to Jeremiah, who carefully dribbled the ball toward the goal, feeling proud he handled it with such precision. Suddenly, a Gamma Ray player tackled him and he knew he had to pass, but could he kick it hard enough? He followed through with all his might and successfully passed the ball to Eric Rhondo, who squeaked it past the goalie for their first goal. Jeremiah jumped up and down, despite feeling faint from the heat. His in-suit thermometer indicated he was in the danger zone, so he cranked up his air conditioning to its max and hoped for the best. He wished he could wipe the sweat dripping off his brow into his mouth. But despite the discomfort, he had never experienced such exhilaration in his life.

Gathering in the changeroom with his teammates after the game, Jeremiah raised a toast to his team, who had won the match 1-0. All were adamant that two fifteen-minute halves were too short for a competition and planned to petition the local authority for a full ninety-minute game.

"So, what was it like for you, Eric?" Jeremiah asked his best friend. "Do you still believe we should only play the game indoors?"

"What makes it unique playing outside? I'll have to think about that. Like you, I have never been so excited in my life. As I told you before, I honestly thought playing outdoors wouldn't be any different, given we were in our PSSs without the wind and sun on us. But the whole experience felt poles apart, closer to competing in an actual game, similar to the videos we've watched of Manchester United running and carrying the ball up the field with such intensity. Yes, I've changed my mind."

Jeremiah grinned at his friend. Eric's hair was matted to his head from the sweat that only thirty minutes outdoors could generate. His tall, lanky body showed signs of exhaustion: a slump to his stance with his shoulders hanging forward, his neck not quite centred on top of his body, his gait slower and more purposeful. But the glow of satisfaction and delight was evident on his face, in stark contrast to his body, which had taken such a beating from his recent exertions.

As Jeremiah travelled home via the underground Maglev train, he was hit by an epiphany stemming from today's game. He decided to focus his time and energy on re-creating the activities and life experiences that had brought earlier populations such pleasure. Surely, customs and traditions enjoyed in the past could be adapted to present-day climate limitations.

The Maglev travelled so rapidly that the passing blur caused many to feel slightly nauseous. Jeremiah rubbed his stomach and took a sip of water to help soothe his system. Although he appreciated the speed, he wished the ride were more comfortable.

Exiting the Maglev, Jeremiah stepped onto the travelator for the five-minute ride to the inner city of Santos. All inner cities were completely cocooned from the outdoors. A giant air-to-air heat exchanger cooled air from outdoors so the temperature remained an ambient 21 degrees Celsius. Identical amenities and shops were supplied to each inner city, so there was little reason to travel between cities unless visiting friends or relatives. But most inhabitants rarely ventured out of their city of 500,000 people. It was big enough to thrive and live a fulfilling life with friends and family.

Jumping off the travelator near his apartment building, Jeremiah took the high-speed elevator to the 21st floor, texting his parents along the way to notify them he was home.

They each had an office in the apartment equipped with the latest audio and video technology, as did virtually all employees. His dad, Luther, was a geological engineer employed to ensure the safety of the underground structures from degrading over the years. Luther often was required to travel to distant inner cities to supervise reconstruction projects or oversee disaster management, including prevention, preparedness, response, and recovery. Although Luther did not share Jeremiah's preoccupation with the past, he and Jeremiah enjoyed complex video games and both practised martial arts.

His mom, Christina, was a gynecologist, providing online birthing supervision to twenty birthing stations situated across the city. She could provide advice and support to ten births concurrently. Occasionally, she went to a live birth to assist, but this happened rarely. Christina shared with Jeremiah a fascination for the past. They scheduled a monthly movie night in which they would watch a movie or documentary from the 20th century, an era both found intriguing.

Realizing he was starving from his outdoor soccer exertions, Jeremiah entered the kitchen and pressed the button for hot beverage #26, Coconut Dream on the drink dispenser and watched as the foamy liquid filled his cup. There were 35 flavours of this refreshing shake of chemical nutrients that was all anyone needed to consume for the day if one chose a shake which delivered a fibre explosion—activated once the liquid entered the large intestine. Most of the population continued to consume snacks, but they were very expensive to produce and limited in amount. Little time was wasted preparing meals or eating together. The government boasted how efficient life had become.

Feeling full at last, Jeremiah's attention turned to completing the forms that would significantly alter his life once he turned nineteen next month. Unfortunately, Jeremiah's younger sister, Angelica, was using the family workstation, but luckily the family/games room was empty.

He settled into the comfy sofa, took a deep breath, and opened the forms on his tablet. *Where to go, where to go.* Such an important decision. He chatted softly to himself. "Perhaps I'll visit the 1960s. In that decade, protest rallies and debate generated an atmosphere of change, but the momentum didn't last. At least I could talk to those involved about the society they were hoping to create.

"Or, the beginning of the 21st century intrigues me, when it was clear climate change was real and happening, but very little was done; why was that? I wonder if visiting that era would help me understand why the political leaders virtually ignored the problem. Apparently, they considered banning single-use plastic bags a big deal. That's laughable.

"Or, what about the 2030s, when Mother Nature found she could no longer cope with being glutted with carbon, and wreaked havoc on the world with a proliferation of hurricanes, tsunamis, droughts, and rainstorms? Whoa, that time sounds too dangerous. After all, we are indebted to the relatively few survivors of that era for creating a new world in which humans could survive."

A month away, a month away. Where do I want to spend this time?

Jeremiah's parents suggested his first time travel (TT) be limited to two weeks, but he was taking advantage of the entire month allotted for an initial TT opportunity at the age of nineteen. Every five years thereafter, a person could choose to TT, extending the time away to a maximum of six months. Workplaces were obligated to offer a leave of absence for these trips.

As Jeremiah entered the terms "September 6, 1965" and "Vancouver, British Columbia, Canada" into his online application, he was light-headed and joyous at the same time. Once he hit send, he texted Eric, asking, "Up for celebration tonight? I did it. Off to the 1960s in September. Stunned."

"Totally gamma, my friend. See you at Atomica at eight. Brave, or what?"

Once the application was vetted, training began immediately. The first TT training lasted one month and was very intensive. A first-time applicant had to pass both a written and oral test before being allowed to travel. Repeat TTs had to train for only two weeks.

As Jeremiah entered the dance bar, Eric, Flossy, and Justine stood up and hollered, "Hey, Intrepid TT— over here."

Jeremiah struggled through the crowded dance bar to his friends. To allow room for dancing, there were no bar stools or chairs, but a small table provided room to rest drinks. He knew his friends had planned a celebration when he saw the lights of one wall spell out, "Jeremiah Phelps, TT to 1960s. We will miss you. Have a hell of a time." The only wall decorations were lights, which were programmed to portray any design the customers requested. Some walls featured designs set to the beat of the music, while others turned into pictures of cats or dogs or current movie scenes.

"How are you feeling?" Flossy asked. "Pretty excited?"

"Almost as high as I can get. But I wish you were coming. I'm going to miss you," Jeremiah said as he kissed her on the nose and hugged her close.

"Are you nervous about the training?" asked Justine.

"A little. I will be so disappointed if I fail."

"You've got this, friend," said Eric. "We believe in you."

"Thanks, Eric. The only module I'm concerned about is the technical side of the time traveller—you know, troubleshooting unexpected complications. I'm not exactly what you would call a techie."

"Remember that virtually every TT goes smoothly," said Eric. "Only three people out of billions of trips have not made it back. But I wish you weren't going alone."

"Yeah, I know. Maybe I should have waited until one of you could come with me, but I want to go as soon as I'm eligible. I can't wait to see what life was like back then."

Two weeks passed before Jeremiah learned whether his application had been approved. Too many contenders had applied for his specific date, so he needed to choose a later date, September 12. No problem. He clicked the Accept key and his training schedule appeared. One week from now, he would relocate to TT Headquarters and live there with other trainees for a month. Then he had a few days at home to say goodbye and his adventure would begin.

Packed and ready, Jeremiah hugged his parents and sister. This was the first time he had been separated from them for a month, although phones were authorized for use in the evenings, once the training for the day was complete.

The first week of training was more relaxed than the following weeks, allowing students to acclimatize themselves to their new living space and face the reality they might soon leave family and friends for a wholly different world. Trainees could relinquish their trip during the initial week of training, but after that, the decision was final, as training was expensive.

Jeremiah was assigned to three modules of training during the first week which focused on assimilation into the culture and the time period he had chosen.

Module One was called Cloning which involved transforming his physical appearance and clothing to fit in with the norms of the people living on the west coast of Canada in the 1960s. As Jeremiah entered the Cloning Room, he was astonished at the immense size of the facility. He thought Cloning Arena might be a more suitable name. The giant domed space was divided into decades, stocking clothes, shoes and boots, with separate areas devoted to hair styling and accessories. Seth had been assigned to alter Jeremiah's appearance in order to blend into the 1960s. The morning started with hair and beard modifications, along with selecting suitable clothing to pack for the trip. Fortunately, Jeremiah had grown his hair longer than usual and attempted to grow a beard, but had only achieved a short stubble.

After two hours of prepping and costume changes, Jeremiah gazed at himself in the mirror and laughed. He now sported bangs and hair that curled around his ears. Seth said his stubble beard was perfect, so he likely wouldn't have to shave while he was away since his beard grew so slowly. He was dressed in brown corduroy bell bottom flares and a checked white and yellow shirt, and had packed polo shirts, slim-cut jeans and a striped sweater. He sent a photo to his parents and friends for a laugh.

Module two involved watching news clips and movies from the 1960s. Jeremiah was fascinated by the Canadian opposition to the Vietnam War. Why would you protest a war instigated by another country? *I'll see if I can attend a protest rally and talk to the demonstrators. How exciting!*

A meeting with his mentor was next. A mentor who had visited the same decade in the same country was assigned to each new traveller. A man in his thirties approached Jeremiah, reaching out his hand to introduce himself. He was tall and lean. His physique suggested he was an athlete.

"Hi, I'm Brent Flavier. Good to meet you." He chuckled as he said, "I had to wear similar clothes and hair. Don't worry, you get used to it when you're amongst others dressed like you.

"Let's go to The House and get a beverage and snacks. You need to try eating solid food as early as possible before you leave. That was a significant challenge for me. I didn't get my system used to solid food before I went and my digestive tract really suffered.

"One option is to take pills with you so you don't have to eat, but you wouldn't believe the time they spend cooking and eating. It's really important to them. Their meal times are extensive and involve families sitting around a table discussing their day. Breakfast is in the morning when you first wake up. Once your taste buds start to come back, you will find Canadian bacon quite tasty. I still miss it.

"Another aspect of their life you may find strange is that families are away from their homes for the bulk of the day, either at work or at school, which differs greatly from our way of life. Most people eat lunch with their co-workers or schoolmates. Dinner, typically the largest meal, is around six at night. As it is considered to be the important meal of the day, family members are expected to be there. They share events from their day, any problems or concerns bothering them, and some families chat about local and world news. It's pretty interesting. You won't see any screens around the table.

"You'll be expected to eat breakfast and dinner with the family who is hosting you. They believe you recently moved to Vancouver (which is true), and are grateful you will be a boarder with them, paying for your room and meals."

They arrived at The House, which served hot and cold beverages and snacks that satisfied those who still needed to nibble. All beverages were composed of chemicals, closely resembling tastes of yore.

"What should I order that was popular in the 1960s?" Jeremiah asked.

"Try an Orange Julius or a root beer. People love them, although I never really developed a taste for them. Their coffee tends to be weak and they let it sit around for too long, so it becomes bitter. I primarily drank water there. They also drink a lot of alcohol. Be careful of that, it can really upset your system and make you drunk easily. You'll have to try some before you go to see how you react, as everyone will expect you to drink what they call 'booze.' Just sip on a drink slowly and try to limit it to one."

Jeremiah ordered a root beer and a bag of pretzels. "I can stomach these," he said. "Why is this a beer if it has no alcohol?"

"No idea, actually," Brent replied. "Why don't you research that before you travel? Do you have any other specific questions in mind, or should I start by sharing my experience?"

"I'm really interested in social change and how a protest movement gets started," Jeremiah said. "I'm hoping to talk to some citizens about how it feels to live in a time of dramatic transformation."

"You will likely find that the average person focused on making a living and raising a family; most individuals were observers of the changes rather than direct participants. If you want to chat with those more directly involved, I suggest you attend a protest, go to a folk concert, visit women's rights organizations, and sit in on a few political studies classes at the University of British Columbia. Try to go where the action is. I think you'll learn more."

"What did you like best about that time, and what did you find challenging living there? I understand you went for six months."

"This was a time in which the focus of society moved to youth. The old ways of thinking were being challenged, particularly in the areas of civil rights, racism, and women's equality. I enjoyed the optimism of youth, believing society had the capacity to change so as to provide a better life for everyone. There was a sense that life could be richer, more exciting, and fun for most folks. But, of course, the pendulum often swings too far in a time of unrest. I found people's opinions were often firmly on one side or the other; there was little room for grey and therefore less opportunity for thoughtful discourse on both sides. I tried to stay out of some discussions because it was clear neither side was going to budge. But on the whole, it's an exciting society to visit.

"In terms of preparation, I suggest you focus on beefing up your digestive system to devour a considerable amount of food, and read widely about the reasons for protest and debate."

Jeremiah felt slightly nauseous from the root beer and pretzels. He vowed to snack every day before he left on his mission, not a usual practice for him. "I think I'm well versed in the reasons for social change, as I've studied that era extensively. What I hope to experience is being part of a radical movement which is currently happening. I hope I can do that."

Brent nodded. "If you have any other questions, call me and we can have a chat or meet. I'm available until you head off."

"Thanks, Brent. I'm also going to read your Experience Report to get a more in-depth understanding of your impressions of the culture." Talking with Brent added to the exhilaration Jeremiah was feeling about embarking on this remarkable journey.

Week One was complete. He still had the weekend to decide if he was totally committed. There was one burning question he needed information on before making that final decision. Jeremiah wondered if there was a significant carbon footprint created by time travel technology. How much fuel was consumed to travel through space?

Jeremiah had an hour to kill before his meeting with his trip advisor, Skylar Bono. They would review his week and ensure Jeremiah was physically and mentally prepared to take this trip. Getting some exercise would help burn off some of his nervous energy, so he went to the gym to run on the treadmill and reflect on how he would word his question. Having showered and feeling refreshed, he walked over to Skylar's office.

"Hi Skylar, I realize the mechanics of TT will be covered next week, but before I make my final decision, I want to know to what extent our travelling contributes to climate change. How much carbon is emitted on a single trip?"

There was a pause before Skylar answered. "We've been working very hard over the years to reduce the carbon released by TT. The launch from our time period emits virtually no carbon, but the entry into the new time period has proven to be problematic. On arrival, the time traveller is definitely adding to the carbon footprint at that end. Let me find you a comparator. Here's one. Carbon released on a single trip is equivalent to flying from Vancouver, Canada to Rome, Italy, in the 1960s."

"So, what you're telling me is we're not contributing carbon to our own atmosphere, but we are increasing the carbon at every destination we visit?"

"Yes, that's about it. But we are desperately trying to reduce it."

"Do you tell all time travellers about this problem? Do they realize they are making climate conditions worse for the world they are visiting?"

"No, we only respond to questions directly related to climate change, such as yours. Remember that TT is the one thing most humans look forward to. It gives them hope and a reason to survive. You've seen the faces and emotions of the returnees. Spending time outdoors for extended periods amongst trees and clean water, even swimming in it, revives them and helps them get through the next five years, when they can take another trip. The mental health of our planet depends on these trips."

Jeremiah was silent and scratched his head, a gesture used to allay nervousness. "Okay, you've given me a lot to think about. Thanks for being so honest about it. I'll let you know my decision by the end of day."

"Please don't discuss this with many others. We don't want it to be general knowledge, if possible. In particular, don't tell other trainees."

Jeremiah called Eric and asked if he could meet with him today.

"Hey, friend, I'm at work. Can't it wait until tomorrow?"

"No, it can't. Can you get away?"

"Okay, let's stroll through the Causeway to get some exercise, and then I can get back to work quickly. Meet me there in an hour."

After explaining the carbon dilemma to Eric, Jeremiah said, "I believe our population is nearing one billion humans on Earth, after incentives were provided to increase the birth rate. If everyone took a trip every five years, over 500,000 people a day would be travelling. I'm going to look up the actual number. In the last month, about 475,000 individuals have left every day. I wonder what those carbon emissions add up to?"

Eric shook his head. "That's truly upsetting information. Don't you think it ought to be released to all the TTs? I mean, we're damaging the Earth's atmosphere, making life on Earth, both in the past and in the future, significantly worse by time travelling. It shouldn't be used for recreation."

"I know this sounds daft, Eric, but is there a possibility our time travel caused the four-degree warm-up that destroyed most of the world in the early 2500s? What would have happened if there had been no TT? Is it possible events from the future can alter the past? I don't see why not. We've been adding tonnes of carbon to their worlds for centuries. What if we caused the tipping point for climate change? Does that sound feasible?"

Eric stopped walking and looked down in thought. "Who can we talk to who might take us seriously? Clearly, no one in the training program is going to welcome our discussion. What about our physics prof Clarity Frieson? She might talk to us."

"Let's book a time to see her next week. Clearly, I'm going to renounce my trip, as much as I hate to. I'm unbelievably disappointed, but I can't, with a clear conscience, go now." Jeremiah felt a cloud of sadness descend on him. "I feel betrayed. How can our government, in good faith, knowingly contribute to climate change without fully informing all the travellers beforehand?"

Jeremiah decided to broach the subject with his parents and sister, as they would want to understand why he had turned down his precious trip. He texted them and asked to meet in the games room.

"I've decided not to become a time traveller and I want to explain the reasons for my decision. But first, I need to know if you are aware of how much carbon is released into the atmosphere when you arrive at your destination."

His parents, Luther and Christina, looked at each other, wondering how each would respond. Angelica, his younger sister, just shook her head. "No idea."

Finally, Luther spoke. "I believe most travellers don't find out about it until after their third or fourth trip, but by then, they are hooked on the rewards of TT. You're right; perhaps if everyone knew prior to their first trip, they would decline it as you have done. But once you've had the opportunity to be outside for extended periods of time, breathing in the fresh air and the amazing smells and experiencing the wonder of hiking through forests and on snow-covered mountains, it's very difficult to give it up."

Christina added, "Once we found out we took turns travelling, so now we only go every ten years. We've always said it's because we have kids and want to spend more time with you, which is true, but the primary reason is the carbon output. No one ever talks about it, but we believe almost everyone knows."

"Eric and I are going to meet with our physics prof next week to talk about the possibility the billions of trips we have taken to the past might have caused climate change to accelerate. If we stop time travelling now, could we reverse some of the damage so our climate might improve?"

"Even if that were the case," said Luther, "our culture revolves around TT. Our economy is based on everyone taking these trips. So many people are employed in the training, technology and advertising involved. Studies comparing our mental health before and after travelling confirm that our mental health benefits significantly from the opportunity to visit another culture and spend time safely outdoors. Most people centre their lives on TT. Remember, there is nowhere else to go on the planet. All the underground cities are identical. If TT were stopped, what would everyone look forward to?"

"Maybe it's time to live in our real world, to face the truth," Jeremiah said. "Perhaps concentrating on the world we live in would lead to new inventions and make us excited about our own world, rather than just waiting to TT. Playing football outdoors made me realize there is so much more we could do to enjoy the world we have. And if we stop TT, our climate is likely to improve—to what extent we don't know, but imagine if the climate were altered sufficiently to plant some trees and extend our time outdoors. How can we morally keep polluting the Earth, destroying it even more to entertain ourselves in worlds that are not ours? It's time to act."

"Good luck, son," said his parents with little enthusiasm. "It's worth a try."

"I wish some of the leaders from the 1960s could TT here to help stimulate a change in thinking," muttered Jeremiah under his breath as he left the room.

ACKNOWLEDGEMENTS

Many of these stories were written in response to writing exercises we challenged ourselves with in our writing group, the NIWBies. It was at this writing group that I started writing regularly and where I realized how important writing is to me. In particular, I want Wendy Reynolds to know how much I value her encouragement and feedback over the years.

A huge thank you to my early readers, Sue Chamberlain and Mary Golbourne for your detailed review of my early draft. Your generosity of time and thought is much appreciated.

I'm also indebted to my editor, Kathleen Byrne, who is so skilled and whose feedback improved the novel immensely.

Also, thank you to Starbucks who provided great coffee and a very pleasant writing environment.

And, of course, giant hugs to my dear husband, Michael, who patiently put up with all my musings and time away writing.

ABOUT THE AUTHOR

Susan Cross is fascinated with short stories. So much is said in such a short time. They capture the essence of a person's life in a few pages. Short stories often show how creative people can be in solving the challenges they face. My favourite short story collection is *Various Miracles* by Carol Shields. Great short stories make the reader think about their own lives and how they would deal with the dilemmas faced by the characters. The story stays with you.

Susan is also unable to resist the call of a mystery book. Take a look at her first mystery novel in a series, *Double Crossed*, featuring Lucy Christie, an amateur sleuth. It's a lot of fun.

The second novel in the Lucy Christie series will be released in early 2024. Watch for it!

Susan lives in Ontario, Canada, with her loving husband, Michael.

www.ingramcontent.com/pod-product-compliance
Lightning Source LLC
Chambersburg PA
CBHW050943050726
47592CB00007B/2409